Flynn Tales

Flynn Tales

Stories by Elizabeth (Bess) Flynn & James (Jimmy) Flynn

Edited & Compiled by

Linda L Flynn

www.journeytotheheights.com

The background cover map came from Alabama Maps, which is an ongoing project of the Cartographic Research Laboratory, operating under the auspices of the College of Arts and Sciences at the University of Alabama.

Permission to use this map for my book cover was granted on November 30, 2016, by the owner of the map, Wayne Remington, with the Enterprise Owner being the University of Alabama. The original map was created by Henry Cuthbert Tunison with the description "World on Mercators Projection."

ISBN: 978-1-7321864-0-8

DEDICATION

This book is dedicated to the memory of Flynn ancestors and to all Flynn's who recognize in themselves the spirit of adventure and love of life reflected in these writings.

Table of Contents

DEDICATION v

ACKNOWLEDGMENTS xi

Introduction xiii

Part One 1

Swan Song 1954 Trip to Europe 3

Departing Home 5

Saturday, March 27, 1954 5
Sunday, March 28, 1954 5
Monday, March 29, 1954 5
Tuesday, March 30, 1954 5
Wednesday, March 31, 1954 6
Thursday, April 1, 1954 6

Ship Travel 7

Friday, April 2, 1954 7
Saturday, April 3, 1954 7
Sunday, April 4, 1954 7
Monday, April 5, 1954 8
Tuesday, April 6, 1954 8
Wednesday, April 7, 1954 8
Thursday, April 8, 1954 8

Ireland 11

Friday, April 9, 1954 11
Saturday, April, 10, 1954 11
Sunday, April 11, 1954 12
Monday, April 12, 1954 12
Tuesday, April 13, 1954 13
Wednesday, April 14, 1954 morning 13

Thursday, April 15, 1954 morning 14
LATER. 14
Friday, April 16, 1954 14
Saturday, April 17, 1954 morning 14
Easter Sunday, April 18, 1954 15
Easter Monday, April 19, 1954 16
Tuesday, April 20, 1954 17
Wednesday, April 21, 1954 17
Thursday, April 22, 1954 17
Friday, April 23, 1954 18
Saturday, April 24, 1954 18

On To London **21**
Sunday, April 25, 1954 21
Tuesday, April 27, 1954 22
Wednesday, April 28, 1954 23

Belgium **25**
Wednesday, April 28, 1954 continued 25
Thursday, April 29, 1954 morning 25

Germany **29**
Thursday, April 29, 1954 29
Friday, April 30, 1954 30
Saturday, May 1, 1954 30
Sunday, May 2, 1954 morning 30
Tuesday, May 4, 1954 morning 32
Wednesday, May 5, 1954 morning 32
Thursday, May 6, 1954, morning 33
Baden Baden 34
Saturday, May 8, 1954 34
Sunday, May 9, 1954 night Munich 35
Tuesday, May 11, 1954 Munich 36
Wednesday, May 12, 1954 morning Garmish 37
Thursday, May 13, 1954 morning 37

Austria **41**
Friday, May 14, 1954 Innsbruck 41
Saturday, May 15, 1954 morning 42
Sunday, May 16, 1954 evening Feldkirch 42

Switzerland **45**
Monday, May 17, 1954 Zurich 45
Tuesday, May 18, 1954 46
Wednesday, May 19, 1954 Lucerne 46
Thursday, May 20, 1954 Lucerne 47
Friday, May 21, 1954 morning 48
Saturday, May 22, 1954 Interlaken 49

France **51**
Sunday, May 23, 1954 Aboard the train to France. 51
Monday, May 24, 1954 Paris 51
Tuesday, May 25, 1954 52

England **55**
Thursday, May 27, 1954 morning Crewe, England 55
Friday, May 28, 1954 PM Chester 57

Back to Ireland **59**
Saturday, May 29, 1954 Dublin 59
Wednesday June 2, 1954 60
Saturday, June 5th, 1954 61
Sunday, June 6, 1954 61

Travel Home **63**
Wednesday, June 16, 1954 63
Thursday, June 17, 1954 64
Friday, June 18, 1954 Montreal 64
Saturday, June 19, 1954 Amherstburg 64

Jimmy Flynn's South Seas Adventure & Other Musings **67**
A Little Background on the Merchant Marines 67

South Seas Adventure **69**

1934-1935 The Trip **71**

Letters to Family **87**

Thursday, 1/17/1935 87
1/21/1935 89
Saturday, 2/2/1935 90
2/17/1935 91
Tuesday, 2/19/1935 1:30 a.m. 92

Friendship #1 Writing **93**

Friendship #2 Writing **95**

Friendship #3 Writing **97**

A Friend's Greeting 97

Friendship #4 Writing **99**

Quotes **101**

Tracked Events **103**

About Linda Flynn **105**

ACKNOWLEDGMENTS

These writings underscore the creativity of the Flynn Family. I can see the family line where my husband and his children drew their creativity from. I appreciate the efforts of former generations (Betty Flynn and John Terrance Flynn) for saving and preserving these documents. And special thanks go to Christine Flynn Platt for both saving these documents and being willing to share them with us, so I could convert them into their current form for others to enjoy.

I consider their efforts important and worthy of acknowledgment, given the current climate of downsizing and minimizing stuff that's embracing our culture. I believe there is richness we can gain from our past and I'm honored to share this history with you.

Introduction

Flynn Tales provide insight into the life of the Flynn family in the mid 1900's. For Flynn descendants these writings may enhance your understanding of your roots. For others, these stories open the door to life for a small business owner & wife and one of their sons. You'll find aspects of life that have changed and attitudes that remain the same.

The main characters in the book are pictured on the cover. From left to right, they are as follows:

John Joseph Flynn (Jack)	13 September 1912/2 May 1990
Elizabeth Mitchell Flynn (Bess)	11 October 1890/15 July 1955
James Anthony Flynn	18 January 1888/27 January 1956
Mary Elizabeth Flynn (Betty)	5 January 1917/1 September 1983
James Mitchell Flynn (Jimmy)	12 February 1911/12 December 1963
Charles Robert Flynn	20 September 1914/4 April 2002

They're standing out front the family business, Potter Manufacturing Company. Located at 6110 N. California Ave., Chicago, IL.

Part One

Swan Song
1954 Trip to Europe

Elizabeth (Bess) Flynn (10/11/1890 - 7/15/1955) and her husband James Flynn embarked on a European trip on March 27, 1954.

For family, the story may impart insight into your distant ancestors. To those who enjoy traveling, the diary will lend first hand accounts of what one might experience during 1954 in Europe. As one who enjoys traveling, these tales left me marveling at the changes that have taken place in travel and spoke to my spirit.

I was surprised at how different travel was in 1954 and Bess's resourcefulness in handling unexpected situations. They left the United States knowing the name of the ship, but not the departure location. Bess and Jim knew whom they would contact upon arriving in Ireland. They'd establish the rest of their plans after arriving there. She traveled places I've been, and places I want to visit. It was refreshing to find a few of her impressions of places similar to my own experience. Her travel diary opens understanding into the world they found in 1954 and insights into her personality. During this trip she mused about a future trip to Italy and Spain — these plans never materialized. This European trip became Bess's swan song.

Departing Home

Saturday, March 27, 1954

Left Canada at noon—after the usual last minute business, etc. Stayed overnight at Berlin Center, Ohio. Dinner at "Mary's."

Sunday, March 28, 1954

Got up early — drove and drove trying to find a church—no luck. Many Lutheran, Evangelical, etc. Breakfast at Howard Johnson's on the turnpike. Reached Washington mid-afternoon—bathed and rested. Turners and Goders arrived about 6. We had some drinks. Wrights arrive—found us by listening. Dinner. Vaccination rash very bad.

Monday, March 29, 1954

Breakfast with Goders. Rumor en re Ryam (Check document to see if it's Rumor en re Ryan) sailing from Baltimore. Trip with wives of convention to Embassies of Luxemburg, Japan, and Mexico. One of Japan charming. Luxemburg overdone and entirely oriental. Mexico had nice murals and sunroom of tile etc. Table in Japan embassy to seat 24 with four additions.

Betty and I had lunch and shopped. Gifts to me of earrings and hose. Ties for Jim.

General Tracy came up. Wrights, Turners, Goders and Flynn had drinks and dinner.

Got on train at 11:00 and slept until 1:00 when train pulled out—no sleep from then on.

Tuesday, March 30, 1954

Arrived New York 7 AM—much the worse for a bad night—cramped bedroom, etc. Called Holland American only to find we must go back to Baltimore on Thursday. Something always happens to us! Bought $1000 American Express checks. Lunch at New Yorker. Dinner at Ruby Foo's—

chicken-almond, etc. Very good. Walked back from 52nd Street to 34th Street & 8th Avenue.

Wednesday, March 31, 1954

Lazy day—nothing had to be done. Went to Macy's etc. Dinner at Joe Kings—17th Street and 3rd Avenue Rathskeller. Good food and fun. Piano Player—old songs—all sing. Jimmie phoned.

Thursday, April 1, 1954

Mass at 7:15. Confession and communion. Then what a day! Packed our bags and were ready at 11:00 train to leave at 12:00. Went to station—were told train to leave at 1:00. Put bags in lockers. Moments later we found the mob! 900 passengers with all their friends, their relatives and their luggage. Hundreds and hundreds of suitcases, plaid clothes bags, grips, boxes, shopping bags (string)—folding go-cards, etc., as well as a large number of harried young men with badges marked "Ryndam." Everyone was asking questions—some were berating the officials as though they were to blame for the dock strike. There was, of course, the woman in tears who could not find her luggage, some whose papers were not in order, etc. Finally we got on board the train. Luckily, one of the "Ryndam's" took us in a back way ahead of the mob—into a car for first class only. Then we waited some more. Later I learned that one baggage car (there were three) had the wrong kind of coupling. Finally, "out of town." Reached Baltimore late afternoon and had a strange, bumpy ride through freight yards and down beside the dock. At any rate there was no long walk. We were there! About 6:30. Our cabin was a happy surprise—room must be 10 x 12 nicely furnished and carpeted, lots of storage space, nice bathroom, etc. Dinner about 7:30, very good and welcome by that time. Luggage showed up later. Unpacked and "off to bed."

Ship Travel

Friday, April 2, 1954

To Mass and communion at 7:00. Irish priest returning to Africa via England. Four nuns, one of whom gave the responses.

Food is very good and of great variety—tendency to overeat.

Met two couples from Jersey City who are interesting, especially Dr. Kelley.

At our table—a young man from St. Louis who is in the paper business, an elderly man from England who is most interesting—had been visiting a son in South Carolina.

Jim went to picture show. Got my exercise by walking round and round the deck.

Saturday, April 3, 1954

Mass and communion at 7:00. Larger crowd today. Warmer today, must be in the Gulf Stream.

Invited by the Captain for party before dinner. Great variety of good appetizers, piping hot, and lots of champagne. All first class passengers invited but Captain sat with our group of eight. Storming at bedtime.

Sunday, April 4, 1954

Storm got worse so we rolled all night and today. I bolstered myself between blanket roll and extra pillow, so didn't roll out. Snow and rain—for all day. Stinky! Mass at 9:30 chairs fell over, altar slid, so it was rather strange! Whole tray of bullion cups etc., went down with a crash. Eating was a hazard—as things slid from end to the other. Canasta game with Dr. Kelley and Mr. and Mrs. Fleckenstein.

Monday, April 5, 1954

Better weather but still rough. Played Canasta before lunch. Passed the Liberty during lunch. Went up to the bridge — ship equipped with all the new devices. Went to a movie in the afternoon—carnival story—terrible. I came out exhausted. Played Canasta again—good game.

Tuesday, April 6, 1954

Mass and communion. Radiogram from Betty and George—later one from Jack Keefe. Chief steward broke the news to our friends. Message from Jack and Charles. Big ado at dinner—fine cake with pale green icing—roses, etc., champagne for our table. Nice evening.

Wednesday, April 7, 1954

So rough we only had rosary. I am exhausted from being thrown around. People who have made many trips say this is the worst. Furniture, which is not fastened, slides entire length of rooms—sometimes with you in it. Jim went the length of the lounge. Played Canasta at night.

Thursday, April 8, 1954

Bad storm—so we are really getting rolled. In the dining salon, dishes, silver, flowers, etc., went sliding off the table, in spite of part of cloth being dampened. Cooks having a lot of trouble as food goes on floor. I might know this would happen to us.

Farewell dinner — as several leaving boat at Cobh, including our six-some. Nice dinner with steak etc., Baked Alaska for dessert — one for each table and very good. The baker on the boat is really a whiz—haven't eaten so many desserts in years. Edw F and I had two games of Canasta very hot. —One each. Lots of fun.

Swan Song

Destinations in Ireland

Ireland

Friday, April 9, 1954

Busy day—letters to write—papers to fill out for landing cards, etc., besides packing.

They served us a special dinner at 5:00 on account of leaving. Wonderful meal with a special cake for six of us—made with fruit, etc. At this rate I will weigh a ton soon.

Arrived harbor about 6:30 but lots of delays—pilot came and took us in to where we met the lighter—people getting on—going through papers—getting cars of the Random etc. The customs etc. Boy from travel bureau to meet us with mail etc. Drove to Cork, Imperial Hotel. Pleasant surprise, big double room with beds, down puffs, lovely bathroom, etc. Towel bar—heater combination super.

Other four arrived late on account of car etc. Jim and I had drink in the bar, then drinks for 6 in the room.

Saturday, April, 10, 1954

What a day!

Had breakfast with the sextet—then Shannon rep came up. Got my driver's license, papers for car, etc. He had said last night that he would be with us to Tralee. But we drove a few blocks from hotel—he put me at the wheel and had me drive him back thru traffic to get his train to Limerick. Here was I—on the right hand side of a strange car—which shifted with my left hand—driving up the "wrong side" of the street as narrow as the ones in Amherstburg and with more turns than a fish worm. There are no numbered roads so I guessed my way. Once I got out of Cork, which is quite a city, I was not so nervous, and got along OK. But believe me, I will never forget it. Ireland is more rough than I thought—not one straight piece of road. Huge rocky peaks—and along the lower hills were millions of brilliant yellow bushes. Spring flowers are in bloom—daffodils, etc., millions of multicolored primroses and many flowers I do not know. We came over the mountains to Killarney—then on to Tralee. The towns are very strange—rows and rows of "flats" which look like housing projects of a hundred years ago. The only fine buildings seem to belong to the church—colleges, etc. People are poorly dressed (cotton stockings) and not too clean. All buildings are at the sidewalks—with small back yards. In the rural areas everyone has a burro. A few have one horse, with a two-wheeled cart which has no springs—just some boards to put stuff on. We are within a block of the church where Jim's father was baptized. The hotel is a dandy—the floors slope in every direction—there is no heat (finally got an electric heater)—no private bath etc. There are some nice antiques.

Sunday, April 11, 1954

Had a happy surprise when we came to bed—had been sitting by the fire downstairs. In each bed, with pajamas around it, was some kind of heater. They look about like a quart flask and were too hot to handle at first, but stayed pleasantly warm until morning. We were warm as toast. I know now why the Irish have such large families—they stay in bed to keep warm.

Went to Mass at 8:00—seemed strange to be going to the church of Jim's grandparents. It is a beautiful church, fine windows, etc. But benches and dirt floor. More and more this place makes us think of Mexico—all the old women in shawls—dropping their pennies in the box. Instead of palm today, we just had some sort of coniferous tree broken in pieces. I think in Mexico we had olive. The church is very large and each Mass crowded—I guess everyone is Catholic.

Went to soccer game—semifinals for high schools—like our all-American—best players from various teams. Good game and interesting crowd. On the way back—stopped at the White Lamb for a drink. No ladies room so sat on a bench in a place about 3 x 6—three men, Jim and I.

Rosary and benediction at 7:00. Talked to Mr. Doyle, the sacristan about records. He is very funny but most efficient. In 30 minutes had had most of the records. Jas. J. Baptized Jan 12, 1859.

Monday, April 12, 1954

More records in re: Maggie and Anthony. Drive thru Killarney into the lake area. Very rugged country.

Kelley's and Fleckenstein's arrived 6 PM, so we had dinner.

Mr. Doyle took us to Fenit, port on Tralee Bay. Excerpts from letter from Benner's Hotel, Tralee, April 14:

"Wish I had my car—you should see me tootling down the road in a Ford, right hand drive—left hand shift. Wrong side of a road about as wide as our driveway. When I hit 40 I feel like I was doing 100.

Food so far is OK—plain meat, potatoes, bread and butter, but palatable. Beds are good and at night we have a foot-warmer in each bed. Only fire is in the lounge. But it is OK and we are enjoying ourselves. Jim is having the time of his life—but gets very tired trying to do things."

In Killarney—went through the estate of Earl of Kenmore, 10,000 A.

I find Ireland is never cold—vegetation semi-tropical, palms, etc.

Tuesday, April 13, 1954

Saw Msgr. Rediy—no further information. Market day—cattle running all over the streets. Went over and talked to John Kelley—old-timer and very interesting. Told of people going to States for 3 pounds—had to carry a bag of straw for bed, and food for 6 or 7 weeks.

Drove to Castle Island—went to convent where John Flynn baked! Sisters were so hospitable—served wine and cookies—even though Holy Week here is really strict.

Met a funny man in a bar. Told of a drunk taken home by friends. On him, they put 'winkers'—bridle to us, with bit in his mouth. Took him to his wife who got the brush (broom). He says: "The one for the road is the one that gets you." Finale: a prayer that we mightn't die in sin.

Returned Irishman from the States, on being told whiskey had gone from 4 pence to 8—said: "Sure, I'll follow it to a shilling."

Wednesday, April 14, 1954 morning

Finished up with Msgr. Ready, as to Masses, etc. Left Tralee at 12:30 drove through Listowel, Tarbert—along the Shannon River, which is so wide it is more like a bay. Beautiful drive. Saw ruins of castle—several stories high—must have been some place. Arrived Limerick 4 PM. Tried to see Nell's cousin, but after visiting three convents found she was 20 miles away, so gave up. Fine room in Crouise Hotel—about 20 x 24—1 double and 1 single bed. Lots of nice furniture, fireplace, etc. Bathroom big as a bedroom. I sure made use of it. Excellent dinner in grill room. Went to St. Augustine, Tenebrae. Very impressive—lights out one by one. Gift for Nell.

Thursday, April 15, 1954 morning

Went to communion at 8. Had mass said for Nell. Good breakfast.

LATER.

Lovely day and tonight I am exhausted. Left Limerick this noon and drove to Galway—better roads—better homes, etc. Many old castles. Went to Shannon Airport when we left Limerick and watched the Yankee Clipper arrive. Fine airport with service of so many airlines. Signs in English, French and Gaelic, (which is worse than Chinese).

Galway is a large city—but not very inviting except view of Galway Bay.

Road became better as we came toward Athlone, which helped, as roads so far had been so narrow and crooked that after fifty miles we were exhausted. While in Galway I asked about hotel en route to Dublin—and found the Shamrock. It is just outside Athlone—in enormous grounds - flowers, etc. It is an old family home made into a hotel. Lovely furniture etc. There are 30 bedrooms. Of course, new plumbing, etc., has been installed. The food is super, so after a fine meal I am in front of the fireplace, at peace with the world.

Friday, April 16, 1954

Drove to Dublin, stopping to visit some churches in route. Dublin is a madhouse—they can have it back—just a big, dirty city—traffic has no sense. No traffic lights and few police and they are stupid. The hotel is comfortable, but mostly style—service or food not so good as Limerick or Athlone. Six guys in the dining room in tail coats, etc., and it takes 20 minutes to get a glass of water. Took a ride for an hour but not much to see.

Through the country, coming from Athlone, there are some big estates—but homes are 1/2 to 1 mile from the road, and with 6-foot stonewalls—so you can't see much.

Went to Tenebrae at night—very long—but wonderful voices.

Kelley's and F's are here.

Saturday, April 17, 1954 morning

Mail from home—letter from J.M.F.—sent to Limerick—and sent here before we got to L. Two letters from office, and just now letter from Betty, so I know everyone is O.K.

Turned in the car—and glad to get rid of it. I will surely appreciate American cars and roads.

No news in re boat home—so can't make plans until after Tuesday.

They really observe Good Friday etc., here—all stores closed all day. Also Monday is a holiday—and Saturday is about the same. Traffic is terrible—all the people are going somewhere.

Saturday evening went to a new place for dinner—MacMullen had told me—rather strange place to find here, as it is French—even to the menu. The name is Jammet's and it is a very good place. Nice atmosphere—not very big, but nice people, dining nicely.

Easter Sunday, April 18, 1954

Went to Mass at 8—thought I was back in Mexico—people coming and going etc. The Pro-Cathedral is round, which makes it worse, with at least 8 doors, etc. Very short mass—no sermon, two priests giving communion all around the round alter rail during Mass.

Sat around after breakfast until 11:30 when the En Tostal parade began. The opening ceremony, by Mr. O'Kelly, the president, was a block down the street. Then the parade lasted an hour—lots of "military"—tanks, soldiers, marines, etc. They were well dressed and drilled and made a much better showing than I expected. Maybe the Irish just like to fight.

After the military part, there was some sort of historical pageant—each of the 32 counties having people in historic costumes—some on horses, in chariots, etc. Since I know nothing of their history I got little out of it.

Then came the flower parade, which was good—lots of floats all covered with flowers, pretty girls, etc. Since the spring flowers are in full bloom it was lovely.

Right after the parade we got a call from the K's and F's — who had driven out to a country club—found out it was nice and wanted us to join them. Got a cab and went out—about 8 miles along the coast. The club is open to anyone—nice course and beautiful clubhouse. It used to be the home of Jameson, of Jameson's Irish Whiskey; they have room for 60 "guests." The place faces on the Irish Sea—with a really super beach—would sure like it in summer. Food was very good, also the service. The grounds are full of flowers.

After we ate, all 6 got in F's car and drove until 6:00 thru the valley of the Boyne River—the best land, etc., so far. Large fields of winter wheat or ?—orchards all in bloom, and fine new buildings. It was a treat to be in a car again. Ed has a '54 Hudson.

Last night 6 of us went to dinner at the Royal Hibernian Hotel—nice old hotel—and good atmosphere. But shade of St. Patrick—hotel by the name—and menu all in French! It should have been in Gaelic! We had an excellent dinner with a bottle of good wine. Mr. F. has lived in Bavaria and is quite an authority on wines, also foods. He spends 3 months every other year—so knows the way around. He has told us so many things—to make European travel easy.

Living (rooms and board) are very cheap over here. Table d'hote meals run from 5 to 12 shillings—$.70 to about $1.70—very few of the latter. At the Portmarnock Club yesterday—our two dinners cost 15 shillings—$2.10 and that includes the 10% tip.

Easter Monday, April 19, 1954

Another wonderful day. Six of us left here this morning and drove down the coast. It is beautiful rolling country in rich land. There are many trees; all coming into bloom, and the whole country is a blaze of color. Rhododendrons are simply fantastic and so many of them. The blossoms start from the ground and many of the bushes are at least 25 feet high and as large around as a room. Daffodils grow practically wild—there are primroses of every color—many bright purple flowers of the phlox sublet type—tulips, etc. The Judas trees—flowering peach etc., are all along the roads.

Houses in this area are nice—so the drives are full of oh's and ah's.

We had lunch at a hotel, which was once the home of Lord Innes. He could not pay taxes etc., and lives in a small house someplace on the property, which has 500 acres. Twenty-five acres are landscaped so it is beautiful. Had a fine meal. Also had a bad scare. Jim, as you know, does not pick up his feet—so caught under a rug and fell so hard he skinned his nose. He seems to make it OK, though, with no bad effects. But is scares the pants off everyone else. Having him hurt or ill in a foreign country would be a problem.

We went to see the Abbey Players—and thoroughly enjoyed it. Of course, local jokes were over our heads, and once in a while there was a bit of Gaelic—but all in all it was most enjoyable. Jim really enjoyed it, as there were lots of laughs.

We had skipped "high tea"—so we all went to the grill and ate and drank until they started turning out the lights.

Tuesday, April 20, 1954

Wrote BFG and JMF

Very quiet day. F's and K's getting away—has bags in our room etc. Jim not feeling well—reaction from fall etc. Ate early and went to bed.

Wednesday, April 21, 1954

Could not get laundry done—so did a big washing—bathroom looks like a Chinese laundry. Thank goodness for nylon.

Went shopping and got quite a lot done. Stores—good ones are some distance from hotel, so I was weary when I got back, only to find the "lift" was out of order. There is only one, so I trudged up to 405, got rid of parcels and rested a bit. Then I went down for lunch (it is the principal meal here, as in Mexico). Now I am up again—and sure hope the lift is fixed soon. I would hate to carry Jim up on my back.

When I went to lunch I got a Real Surprise—Jim had also been out, and he bought me a wristwatch. I was certainly pleased.

Still no plans.

Thursday, April 22, 1954

Big day—in fact, nearly too big.

First of all, Jim wanted to go to Cook's Travel Bureau—where he had been the day before. So, armed with the plans, which Ed F had written, we went. To my surprise, after our dealings with Shannon Travel, we found a pleasant, intelligent young man, who is fixing us up with RR tickets for the trip. We will make a circle tour of London, Belgium, Germany, Austria, Switzerland, France, and return.

Went shopping in a big way. Jim got a fine tweed jacket—even signed by the weaver—also a "weskit," with which he was entranced. I bought a tweed suit, which will be perfect here, as it is damp and one feels chilly. I also bought two nylon blouses.

Went on and bought material for a tweed dress.

This doesn't sound like much—but we walked miles doing it, and were really tired. We also made another trip to Irish Shipping and Shannon Tourist for mail. Came home and change clothes and went out to eat. I don't know if I was just overtired or what happened—but walking home I got a pain and could hardly make it back to the hotel. Went to bed at 8:30 and stayed until 11:00 AM and took no walks.

Friday, April 23, 1954

Had breakfast in bed! Something for me!

Finally got up and did my washing—wrote letters etc. Ate in the hotel and took it easy. Wrote JMF & BFG—office.

Saturday, April 24, 1954

Made the rounds again today. Irish Shipping, Shannon for mail (none) and to Cook's to pick up our tickets. It looks as though we are going around the world!

Tried a new place to eat and it was wonderful—called the Dolphin (hotel) and is over 100 years old. They broil the steaks right in front of you, and they were good, perfectly cooked. We leave tomorrow night—so much pack etc tomorrow and had better go to bed now.

Except from With the Tide, Amherstburg Echo:

> LETTER FROM IRELAND...a letter this week from James Flynn—who with his fair lady—is on a trip to Europe...the letter was dated April 23 from Dublin ...Mr. Flynn wrote:
>
> "We sailed from New York or rather Baltimore as we had to get the boat there a day late, April 2, on account of the strike.
>
> As the boat did not take on much cargo, on account of the strike, it was quite light and bobbed like a cork all the way over but on one was ill in our party. Have 850 tourist class passengers and 40 first class. We arrived at Cobb, Ireland, April 9. Our car and driver met us and drove us to Cork where we had nice accommodations at the Imperial Hotel.
>
> We left next morning for Tralee, County Kerry, where my father and all his 8 sisters and brothers were born. Also my grandparents. And believe it or not their parents were born in Tralee and records show their name was O'Flynn.
>
> We spent 5 days there and around the Lakes of Killarney before we left for Limerick for the evening and next morning. Then drove to Galway and saw the famous Galway Bay we heard sung about many times. From there we drove to Athlone where we were agreeable surprised by the fine rooms and Guinness' Stout at the Shamrock Hotel.
>
> We arrived here on Good Friday for the opening of An Tostal. Easter was a great day here.
>
> We drove about 50 miles to an old mansion for our Easter dinner.
>
> We said for London on Sunday, then to Belgium, Frankfort, Munich, Oberammergau, Innisbund, Austria, Zurich, Lucerne, Switzerland, Paris and return to London and then back here to sail for New York about June 2.

Should have many good color photos to show and tales to tell on our return.

Miss the Echo but will take a day off on our return to read your files.

Hope all is well and Amherstburg continues to prosper.

Best wishes. Sincerely.

Jim Flynn"

Destinations in England

On To London

Sunday, April 25, 1954

Mass at 8—breakfast and at the packing. We decided to go very light, so repacked everything. Left most of the stuff at the Gresham. On so many short trips it is not practical to check things, and when I have to handle, I don't want much. I will depend mostly on my suit and blouses.

Took a cab from the hotel out to the pier—a few miles—but rather a pretty drive. Went to the Hotel Pierre—on the beach, had a drink and a very good dinner. Got on the Cambria at 8:30. Plans made by Cook's were to leave boat at 11:40, take a train at 1:10, arrive London 6:30 AM. Didn't sound good to me. The Cambria turned out to be a fine boat, with good cabins, etc. So, we had a nice room with two beds (no upper) private bowl and toilet room. Had a good sleep—good breakfast and got train at 7:30 this morning. Customs man did not even ask me to open a grip!

The trip by train in the daylight was wonderful as we went through such beautiful country. We got to see so much. The RR system here is fantastic—not double track but from 4 to 15 or 20—some places two levels. Every road crosses above the tracks—so there are hundreds of underpasses—and a great many long tunnels. Train is strange—all compartments with six seats. We were first class so had very comfortable seats. They even have two diners, first class and ? We had a fine luncheon but the way of serving is strange. After the soup, waiters come through with huge platters and bowls. You may have lamb (called roast joint), chicken, or fish. After you get your meat, they bring huge bowls—2 kinds of potatoes, carrots, greens, watercress and you take one or all. Same way with dessert—trays of ice cream—apple turnover, etc.

The countryside is beautiful—very neat, with small fields divided by hedges instead of fences—so the whole place looks landscaped.

Every once in a while you see a castle, perched on a hill, some still good, some in ruins. There are countless small towns, which are very picturesque—red tile roofs, up and down the hills. England is full of hills and rocks (that part of the country)—so it makes interesting scenery. There are fine bridges also. Flowers are in full bloom—brilliant red and yellow tulips in huge beds—millions of colored primrose, cineraria, bright purple phlox subulata, (at home there is only pink or white, like Callahan had on the bank). Even here in London, many apartments have window boxes in full bloom. Jim keeps remarking about the flowers.

Had trouble getting a room—but they finally took us in, after a slight delay. The Grosvenor House is immense—fine big rooms and beautifully furnished. We have a big room—must be 20 x 20—one entire wall is cupboards of every kind—with shirt drawers, shoe racks, etc.; huge bath and an entry, where you put your shoes for the porter, etc. The hotel faces Hyde Park, of which more later.

After a good bath, we went out for dinner, at the Trocadero, which is a very old place—goes back to the gay nineties. Takes up about a block, with various dining rooms. Had a good dinner, a good dance band playing, and a lot of atmosphere. Even the simple places go in for waiters in tail coats, etc., and make a ceremony of a simple meal.

Called Mrs. Sullivan and they are coming at 6:00 on Tuesday.

Tuesday, April 27, 1954

Had breakfast at Hotel Connaught—near the American Embassy. Nice air about the place—seems to be a favorite with Americans.

Walked around the stores on Oxford Street. Some are nice—but most are not! London seems small—as so many people are crowded into a small area. Our hotel is at Hyde Park—yet an easy walk to the banking and shopping areas.

Took a bus tour and never again! I was OK but it is too hard for JAF. They get you on and off the bus, walk you here and there—and it is too swift a pace. We did a lot, though—saw a lot from the bus—a museum—Houses of Parliament—and "did" Westminster Abbey.

The Sullivan's arrived and we got along fine. He is witty and she is very nice. We sat around the room for an hour or so—with a drink. I felt like a sot—Jim with Stout—and the others with sherry. However, I refuse to be ill just to be polite. We went to the Regent—address Piccadilly Circus—for dinner. Good food and good music. Of course our tongues went a mile a minute. Party broke up early as they have some distance to go and we have to be up early. To my surprise, the Sullivan's both kissed me quite thoroughly—so I guess I got by. We are to see them on our return.

Note: Ultimate in luxury: Sheets and pillowcases are all of really superb linen.

Excerpt from letters from London:

> "Food at the Trocadero was good—but really, they have no meat—lots of fowl and fish. When Jim asked for steak, the waiter just looked sad and shook his head!"
>
> "Had my hair cut in Tralee and here, 2 shillings, Meat fine in Ireland. Not much here. Had mutton on train and fish and lobster last night."

Wednesday, April 28, 1954

Trip by train from London to Dover—saw nice country but two things to remember: miles of hop fields—with poles 10 to 12 feet high and miles of string for vines. Also cone-shaped houses for drying the hops.

I have heard for years of the "White Cliffs of Dover"—Now I know what they meant: Pure white cliffs rising out of the sea, as you leave, or return. Boat from Dover to Ostend.

Destinations in Belgium

Belgium

Wednesday, April 28, 1954 continued

This is the cleanest country I ever saw—very prosperous—everything so neat. The farms have nothing unsightly—houses and all buildings are in good repair. All brick, in various shades of pink and red—woodwork painted very bright blues, greens and red, with white outlines—very striking. Poorer ones are whitewashed. Fields—small or large—bordered by trees set like posts but growing.

Thursday, April 29, 1954 morning

This is a nice country, sure better than England. Everyone and everything seems prosperous. We are at the Hotel Metropole—which is worth a trip here—it is simply magnificent—but in good taste. The first floor walls are all soft toned brown marble. The carpets are fine and have such original patterns! The dining room is the most beautiful room I have ever seen—there is so much gold it looks like a Mexican church—but the colors are so subdued it is not garish—soft tans and buff that blend with the marble—with a very soft blue in small places just for contrast. The chandeliers of "silver gilt" and crystal look as though they should be in a museum. Our room is a honey—very large with so much cupboard space. Spreads and drapes for window wall are pastel pink velvet—with blue grey walls with just a tiny bit of pink. Sounds strange but it is lovely. Balcony has magnificent view.

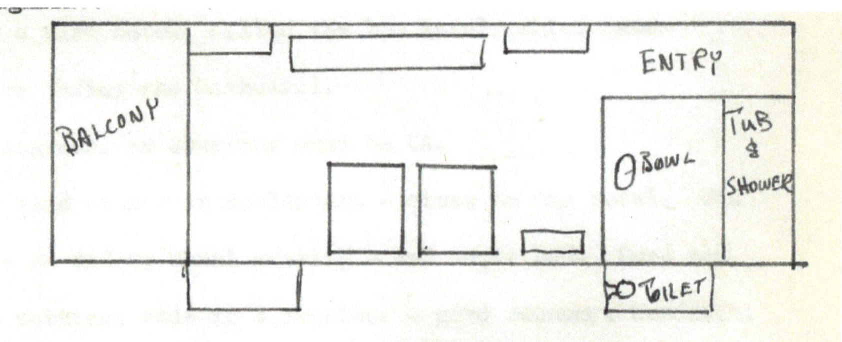

Our room at Hotel Metropole

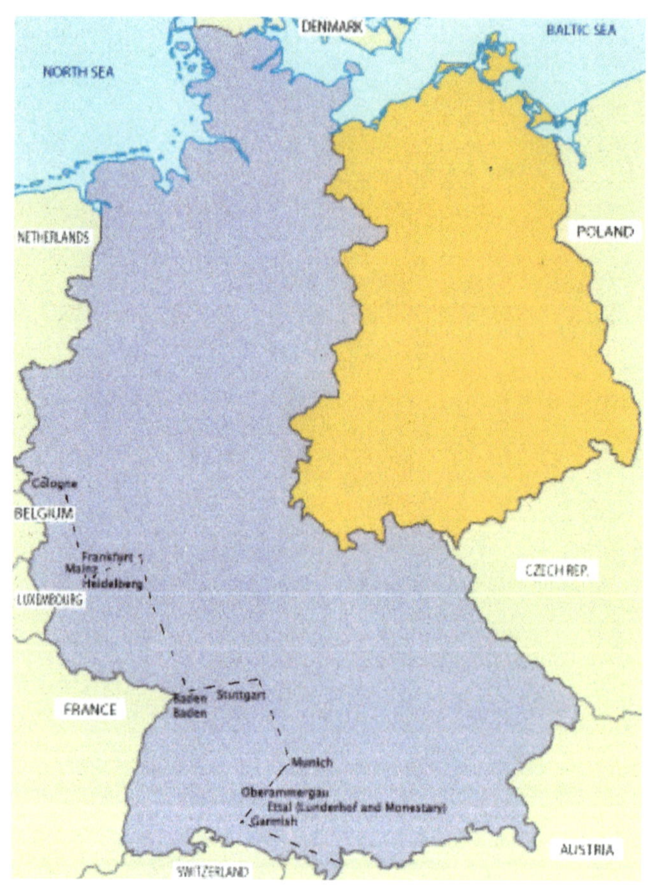

Destinations in West Germany

Germany

Thursday, April 29, 1954

Left Brussels at 11:30 for Cologne. These trains are all strange. This one has two double seats facing each other—big window. Luggage racks over back of seats—double deckers, big enough for suitcases etc. Everyone eats on the train. Well-dressed men, who look like bankers, etc., open their briefcases, take out sandwiches etc. Of course, some people have a big roll with "filling," while some have "finger" sandwiches with crusts cut off. Also, a boy comes through with coffee, cake, etc.

Changed trains at Liege. A nice young man helped us off—told the porter where to take us, etc. There are no "train" porters - so I have a bit of a job getting off. On the train coming to Cologne a fellow wanted me to smuggle a pound of coffee into Germany. However, he got off before customs came on. The man who handled our passport cards came in and sat in our compartment. We had quite a visit and when customs man opened the door, our friend just waved him out. So that was our getting into Germany. Then when we reached Cologne he got a porter to come aboard and get our baggage and take it to the hotel—a block away. Service!

It is a nice hotel, called the Dom Hotel, which means Dome, as we are facing the Cathedral.

No telegrams, so everyone must be OK.

Had a good dinner at Schlenters—close to the hotel. Was rather weary—so did my usual washing—and go to bed. Good bed, but strange—mattress made in 3 sections—good economy. Wonderful down puff glorified pillowcase—tucked in at the foot so it doesn't slide. The case is also your top sheet—so puff is always clean. It is so light and still good and warm.

Friday, April 30, 1954

Had breakfast—wonderful rolls and dark bread. Went to Cook's and got lined up for trip tomorrow. Exchanged train tickets for steamer and will go by water from here to Mainz, a few miles from Frankfurt. We will have a cabin and sleep aboard tomorrow night—then go to Frankfurt. My customs man told me about the trip and it sounds wonderful.

We hired a car and saw the town—even after ten years the sights make you ill. This was a town of 900,000 people—at the end of the war, 200,000. About 250,000 were killed and the rest went away to find safety. Now it is back to 600,000. With Marshall aid there are 120,000 new homes. People live and also carry on business in parts of buildings—one whole sidewall will be gone, or maybe the two top stories. It is unbelievable.

Bought a small duffel bag, as we keep accumulating stuff.

Lunch at a fair place—in the open. Dinner, good, at Weesels, next to Dom Hotel.

Saturday, May 1, 1954

Up at the crack of dawn, and couldn't close the crack, etc. On the steamer at 7:00. It is a large boat, built to hold 2800 people on excursions. So far as I can see there are four cabins—we have one. This is a wonderful trip, but a bit too long.

Sunday, May 2, 1954 morning

Too tired last night to finish, so here goes. My eyes are still tired from trying to see everything on both sides of the river. This Rhine valley is certainly a vacationer's paradise. No wonder the Romans came in here and built castles, bridges, etc. There are many sections where there are spas, so many hot springs that the ground is warm and they grow wonderful crops. Of course, the main thing is fruit, mostly grapes and apples. It is very mountainous and they plant grapes on the slopes in terraces, with stonewalls to hold the soil. They are so steep I cannot see how they work. There will be hundreds of small plots on one slope. The apples and some others are in full bloom—so it is a great sight. The entire countryside is a huge flower garden. There are hundreds of old castles—some in use, but mostly ruins. But it makes it all very picturesque.

Yesterday, May 1st, is a holiday in this country—so everyone was out. There is a highway on each side of the river—they were full of cars, buses, and motorcycles—hundreds of tents with people out for the weekend. This is an enormous river and there are thousands of tugs, scows, etc. (A tug tows several scows at a time.) Then yesterday the water was full of rowing teams and boats. Many had 8 or 10 rowing in unison, or there were 15 or 20 boats in a group with 2 in a boat. The boats look like the ones in Hawaii, dugouts, I think they were called.

At every stop, anywhere from 50 to 200 people go on or off—it was a mad scramble. Some got drunk, many sang, everyone ate. Meals were excellent, to my surprise, with such a mob.

In connection with May Day, I forgot to mention the procession the night before, when they carried the statue of "Sancta Maria" from one church to the Cathedral. They estimated there were 10,000 in the procession—mostly men—with the streets filled with those who didn't march. There were hundreds of lighted candles being carried—so it was most impressive.

We got off the boat in Mainz this morning—got a train to Frankfurt. We were ushered into a compartment with two colored GI's. One was from Oklahoma, the other from West Virginia. The boy from West Virginia was nice, the other not so nice. They helped us off, got us a porter, etc. We are at the FrankfurterHof—very swank hotel. We have two rooms, each with a single bed (only room they had). There is a connecting bath—in fact a bathroom, with a small room with extra toilet and bowl.

Went to high Mass at 10—church had been beautiful but badly bombed and in process of being restored.

The destruction here must have been terrible—whole blocks still in ruins right in the heart of the city. Many new buildings have been, and are being built, and they are ultra modern.

Had brunch at a fine place, the Kaiser Keller—food excellent. Also, for the first time in my life, I can enjoy beer—what they serve here is entirely different from any other.

Took it easy for a while—got bathed and dressed and went to Kranzler's for "tea." Everyone eats in mid-day, and then has a light meal at night. We like Kranzler's so much—nicely furnished—nice looking people, soft string music, etc.

Talked to Ed F—they are only 40K from here. They are coming in Monday.

Nothing at Cook's so no worries. It is so long since we had mail, I am getting pretty lonesome.

Tuesday, May 4, 1954 morning

Well, yesterday turned out to be quite a day. The four Americans arrived about noon—we had a couple of drinks and then ate here at the hotel. Had a nice lunch with some good wine. Ed thinks he has not had a meal without wine. He ships home 5-600 bottles from here. Dr. Kelley took a nap—Jim and Ed amused themselves someway—women went shopping—but nobody bought anything. At four we all met at Kranzler's for tea. Another Mr. and Mrs. Fleckenstein from Flint, Michigan, had just arrived—flew in from Vienna—so they joined us. Nice couple—he is the Phillips distributor—they have flown all over—Istanbul, Spain, Portugal, etc. They bought oriental rugs in Istanbul, an emerald in Portugal, etc.

Came back to the hotel and four left for Alzenau. The four of us who were left were joined by a Mrs. Fulmer from Pasadena, who had been on the plane. She is a widow and is on a trip around the world, her second. First one was by boat, now by air. But she is taking a year—and stays in one place until she sees everything around—will be in Germany a month or more. Is a very interesting person.

About 8:30 the five of us went out to eat, at Kaiser Keller. Had a wonderful meal and a lot of good conversation. Mrs. Fulmer is full of pep and tells many strange and fun things which happen to her traveling alone.

Did my usual nightly laundry—my underwear and hose and Jim's nylon shirt, and go to bed.

This morning I have bathed—washed my hair, etc. We leave today for Heidelberg.

Wednesday, May 5, 1954 morning

Left Frankfurt at 1:00, nice trip here, arriving 2:30. As usual, nobody on the train to carry baggage—so conductor—(in German) made me understand he would take over. As we pulled into the station—he opened a window (they are wide as two seats), called a porter and handed the bags out the window. We got a cab and came to the Haarlass Hotel. The story we have heard (I do not know German, so it may be wrong) is that years ago, the girls going to the bonnet, which is up the street, stopped here to have their hair cut off—hence the name. It is a lovely spot—right on the river, and is really three <u>old</u> buildings around a courtyard, which is filled with flowers, tulip trees in bloom, etc. The balcony outside one of my windows has a flower box—in vivid colors. At night, in the river in front of us, they have a fountain, with colored lights. It is a pump <u>in</u> the river, so just uses the river water. These people are <u>so</u> ingenious. For instance, we have a door, which can be the bedroom, or the bathroom door.

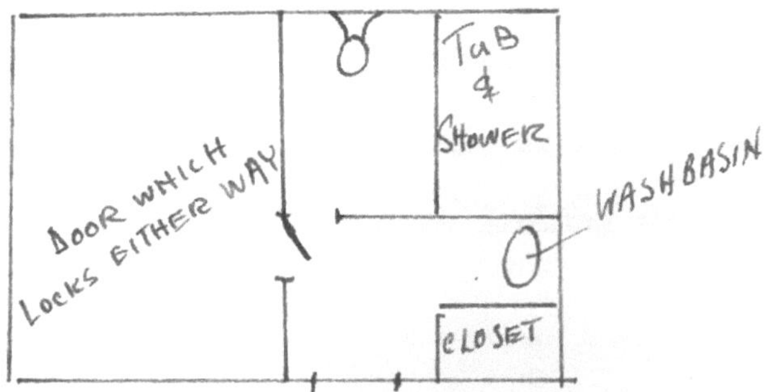

Our room at the Haarlass Hotel

We are really out in the country, mountains and trees behind us—but bus service every half hour. Bus and train service all over this country is far ahead of States.

Dining room is all picture windows and there is the usual garden for eating in nice weather. Picture windows about 6 x 10 are on hinge and <u>open</u>.

Thursday, May 6, 1954, morning

Well, we saw the town yesterday—and did it the hard way. We took a bus into the business section—then walked—miles. Jim can have more fun window-shopping than anyone I know. We had heard of a place called the "Roter Oschen"—Red Ox—so we decided to go there to eat. Took a streetcar—rode and rode. Got there, only to find the place closed. But there was a place nearby, which I decided to investigate. They are so strange—you can't see in, go into a hall and try to find a door—no markings. I just rescued Jim a couple times from the women's toilets. This place turned out fine—<u>real</u> <u>old</u>—and with German families eating. But it was clean and the food was fine. We ordered what I thought was spare ribs and sauerkraut but it was a pork chop and was marvelous. There were only big tables, 6 or more, and the place was about full. After we sat at the only vacant table, an army officer, wife and another gal joined us. He is from Georgia—she from Wisconsin, so we had quite a visit. They were very nice.

Our only purchase for the day was, of all things, a meerschaum pipe. Jim decided to take up smoking one—and so!

Had a bite to eat at the hotel and so go bed.

Baden Baden

Friday morning we took things easy—I wrote letters etc. Left hotel at noon—went by to pick up a pin I had seen the day before. We had decided to come to Baden Baden—our tickets called for Munich via Stuttgart instead. We just go as we please. However the man at the hotel said I would have to get an extra ticket at the station, as the way we were going was a bit longer. Nobody at the windows knows any English—so we just got on the train and told the conductor Baden Baden. He made me understand I must change at Baden Oos. About half way there, we were getting something to eat up ahead, when we came to a station. The conductor came running and pointing—they had hooked our car, with baggage, to another train. We dashed over and got aboard. At Baden Oos—we changed to an electric car—it is only a ten-minute run. However, when we tried to leave (you have to show ticket to get out of a depot) they got all excited and would not let us out. They ushered us into an office and talked a mile a minute, (in German) but I figured out they wanted the extra fare, which was correct, and as soon as I gave them a few marks, all was well. This is a great spa—one of the most famous. Our hotel is very old but nice. We have two single rooms with bath between. That seems to be the thing here, instead of twin beds. The hotel is full of wonderful antique furniture. Each room has a comfortable sofa, (like the one on our back porch). After your "thermal" bath—you can relax. Except we do not take those.

For dinner we went to the "Kurhaus," a simply fabulous place—acres of flowers, shows, cafes, ballrooms, and Casino. The Casino is the most beautiful in the world, (it says here). No movie setting could compare—ceilings two stories high and then a dome—painted with life size figures, etc. The chandeliers of gold and crystal must be twelve feet across and long in proportion. Deep rugs, lounge chairs, mirrors, etc., make it magnificent. I don't know how many tables—but dozens—mostly roulette. You could not even get near a table, so I didn't lose anything.

Saturday, May 8, 1954

Yesterday we walked miles, looking in windows, watching people, etc. When it was time for lunch (2:00 o'clock) I picked out a nice looking place and it turned out to be a honey. They made an omelet with mushrooms, which was a masterpiece. I also had a pastry for which they are famous.

At night went back to the Kurhaus. Had turbot, a wonderful fish, which we had tried in Cologne.

Ordering meals is quite a task—as nobody speaks English in the cafes. I have learned what things are (a lot of them) and though I can't pronounce them, I show the waiter on the menu. Jim is completely at sea, and gets upset at times when we get in a tight spot. But it doesn't bother me; in fact it is fun to get by on my own. By the way, lunch was at the Cafe Konig. And the hotel is Peter's Bad-Hotel sum Hirsch.

Sunday, May 9, 1954 night Munich

Left Baden Baden this morning. Went to Mass at 7:00—on top of a mountain. It wasn't over four blocks from the hotel—but took a cab—as Jim couldn't walk up. I have trouble keeping my mind on the Mass—so much to see, and people all doing something—but never together—some stand, some kneel, and some sit! A lot of the girls are bareheaded which seems strange.

Took a cab to Baden Oos—a few miles—to save getting bags off and on a train for a ten minute ride.

There are so many tracks (one place today our train was on track 21) and trains are going in all directions. Had to buy a ticket and again no English—but finally made myself understood—then found the right track. Had to change at Stuttgart—and getting four bags and Jim transferred is a major operation. However, I have learned to open the window, yell for a porter, and then hand the bags out to him.

The train from Stuttgart to Munich was full of American uniforms—from GI's to VIP's. Talked to some of them, briefly.

Arrived here at 5:00, came to BayrishcherHof and got settled. Took it easy for a bit, and then went to "Franciskroner" for a good meal. Jim had been trying to get ham hocks and kraut every since we came to Germany—tonight he got it—and said it was the best he ever ate. They also served mashed potatoes seasoned with bacon. I had veal, which is wonderful here. Also had Maibock, the spring beer. I like the beer here. Coffee is not good and costs about $.45, so I drink beer.

The owner was talking to us—he speaks a little English and Jim asked him about breakfast. They do not serve until 10:00, and then it is beer and sausage—no coffee.

This is a nice hotel—it used to be very large but one entire wing was bombed. It has not been torn down or repaired. I think there is priority about the work being done. They have put windows etc in one wall, to use rooms.

Instead of "paging Mr. Snitselbaum," a boy walks around with a small sandwich board with your name on it.

Excerpt from letter from Munchen:

> "At all (railroad) stations there are stairs down under the tracks, and up again. There are so many tracks—one place yesterday we were on track 21. But there are walks for the porters—so I tell them Jim can't do stairs—so they take us across. Jim is speechless at what I get done with a few words of German…We go from here to Oberammergau and Garmish—supposed to be lovely. One thing, which is such a constant surprise, is the short distance between cities. Our large cities are 300-500 miles apart—here they are 50 or 60…To go out of our way to Baden Baden, it cost, for two, 7 marks, or about $1.75, roughly. We have a great time with money—Irish shillings, pence, and guineas; English pounds, crowns, etc; Belgian francs; German marks and pfennigs — next we will have Swiss franc then French."

Postal card with views of Munich, mailed from Garmisch, with the following message:

> "Arrived Germany two weeks yesterday. Good weather, good food, GOOD BEER. Leave for Austria today. Both well and enjoying trip immensely. Dad."
>
> From Zurich, the following emerges: "We are in the part of Austria called Tyrol—so many in short pants, long socks, and cocked hats with feathers! We are in the heart of the winter sports area—many hotels not open this time of year, tho they are skiing. The train ride here from Innsbruck was fantastic, up and up, until we were in the snow—at about 4500 feet—with peaks higher by at least that much more—the highest part of the mountains. Lots of tunnels, one 7 miles long."

Tuesday, May 11, 1954
Munich

Yesterday was quite a day. After getting mail at Cooks, in the morning, I got four letters at the hotel, forwarded from Dublin. So I sure felt good.

Munich is really a mess—everywhere you go, there are ruins. The cathedral, which had been magnificent, was badly bombed, but is being restored, as is a smaller church nearby. Since Munich has a cardinal, there are many church offices, etc. I went to mass in a chapel which I think must be the Cardinal's (or Bishop's) private chapel, but which is being used since the church nearby is under repairs. The place was small but exquisite.

We spent some time with Kelley's. The F's had some friends in, and Kelley's did not seem interested. Also a young doctor, who is in service, but who trained in Jersey City, came down with his wife and we had dinner together at the Schwartzwaelder—very good. Back at the hotel, the F's joined us for coffee and dessert in the lounge.

Wednesday, May 12, 1954 morning
Garmish

I was up early yesterday, as we had planned to leave at 8:30, but Jim decided to sleep—too much Maibock the night before. I went with Mrs. F to see about a dress which she is having made—cocktail dress—$150.

We left at 1:30 and came to Garmisch—next door to Oberammergau. It is a storybook town, with the highest mountains of all the area surrounding it. Believe it or not they are skiing while we sit in the sun drinking beer. It is fantastic. The houses and shops are all painted with pictures and fancy decorations so they look like illustrations from a child's book. This is the recreation area for "military"—so the place is full of men, cars, and busses for service personnel, etc. They have taken over one big hotel, on a lake at the foot of a mountain, where the boys stay for $.75 a night.

The hotel, which had been recommended, was closed for repairs we picked another at random—and it is O.K. It is all being done over—but our room and bath are all done. Hotel is full of statues, angels, crucifixes, etc. Very quaint.

We walked the main street, window-shopping, and saw several things I would like. But going via France, England, and Ireland makes the customs too complicated. Will just have to do my buying in Ireland.

At the Hofbrau, met a couple of GI's on leave—got into conversation and they were nice kids—As a result, the four of us went to the Ice Show—which is wonderful. We had heard about it, but it is strictly for the service group. We had drinks, a good dinner and saw a two hour show, arriving home at 12:45. It is a nice place, with tables terraced so everyone can see. We were thrilled to be able to go, and the kids said it was just like being home. They sure get lonely—as we have talked to so many.

Thursday, May 13, 1954 morning

Another very full day! We hired a car, with an English-speaking driver, and spent the day. First we went through fantastic scenery, to "Lunderhof"—a castle built by Ludwig II—the "Mad King of Bavaria." The place is utterly fantastic, small, but with more paintings, mirrors, gold leaf, etc., than you can imagine. In one room are two pier mirrors—several feet high, and the frames are Meissen porcelain, with flowers and birds so well done you feel as though you should smell the flowers. The draperies are either petit point or velvet embroidered with gold thread (one of these weight 80 lbs). The grounds are full of statues, fountains, waterfalls, etc. As the mountain behind is 300 ft higher than the castle, the melting snow furnishes water and pressure. Most castles are in ruins but this one is in perfect condition.

From there we went to Oberammergau. Went through the "spielhaus" theatre—where the Passion Play is enacted. Saw all the props, costumes, etc. It must be a spectacle.

We had lunch at Hotel Alois Lang, son of Anton Lang, who was "Christus" for so long. Had a local dish which was delicious plus chicken fricassee, but with rice and very young asparagus in the gravy.

I took pictures of some of the houses—they are painted in amazing ways. Many have sacred paintings—some flowers. Or anything they fancy! One has the entire story of Red Riding Hood, going around the house; another has the story of Hans and Gretel.

From there we went to Ettal, to see a church, which is in constant use as part of a monastery, which was begun in 1330. It is baroque and overwhelming—so many paintings and so much gold! There are also four caskets of glass with reclining figures entirely dressed in gold set with semi-precious stones.

Came home and relaxed a while—then went to the local hot spot. Tyrolean music and dances—most interesting. The place was full of service men—and we were soon in a group of boys who called us Mom and Pop and we had fun. They had "singsongs" where everyone joined elbows and swayed, etc. I even danced! Women must be scarce! Of course, we knew people they knew—Memphis, Rockford, Utica, Chicago (St. Leo's), etc. We had fun and they were like a bunch of kids. There is a large Intelligence School near here, and many are learning Russian. They said it is very tough. And so to bed!

P.S. All through the country are "field crosses" and small shrines—some quite beautiful. At one point there is a cave about 50 feet above the road; up there, on a natural alter of rock, is life sized, colored statue, of Our Lord.

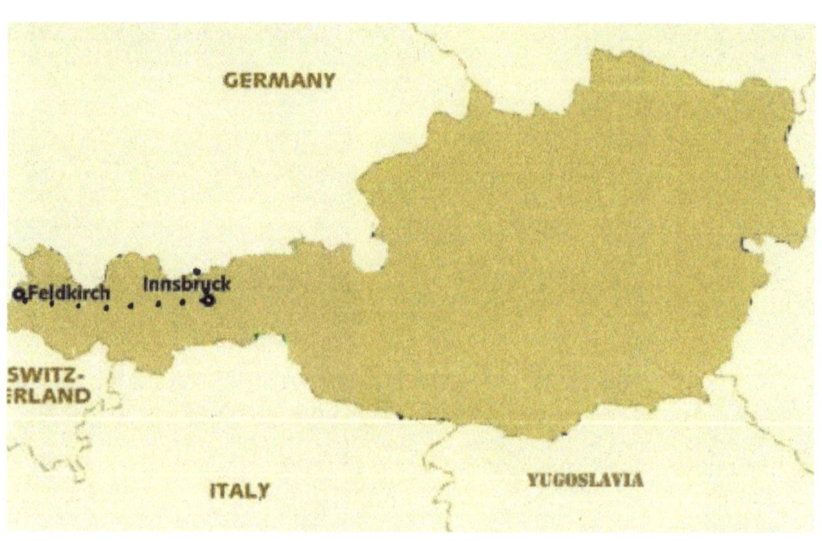

Destinations in Austria

Austria

Friday, May 14, 1954
Innsbruck

Yesterday was a quiet day—both a bit weary from the day before. I walked miles trying to find a magazine or paper, but no luck. Found out I can get them at the US billeting office, but they were closed for the day. They have everything for the men—beautiful tennis courts, bowling alleys, golf course, theatre, etc. It is sure a paradise for the ones stationed here.

The hotel prepared a "special" for us, for lunch, roasted a leg of veal, which was just enough for two. It was excellent. At night I had chicken (1/2) which had evidently been baked in wine—also excellent. We walked again at night and to bed early.

Up early this morning as we left at 10:00. The trip here is really fantastic—snow-capped mountains on all sides—more storybook houses and scenes. All the roofs are red—and when you look down it is quite a picture. We went through countless tunnels—some very long, which go right through a mountain, which is several hundred feet higher than we—and even with tunnels we were up nearly 4000 feet. The trip is short, but takes quite a bit of time, as they stop every few miles. Also we had a long wait at the border. First the Germans checked us out, took up cards, which were issued when we entered. Another German checked our money. Then the Austrians checked passport and money. I guess they make lots of jobs by having a man for each detail. Customs did not bother us at all. Then the Austrian RR checked our tickets. They are all very pleasant but speak no English, so it is hard to know what each one wants. Checked in at the Maria Theresa and have a nice room. For lunch we had some mountain trout — not hard to take. No mail here but hope to get some at Zurich. Will ask again in the morning before we leave. We will go to Feldkirch tomorrow, then to Zurich. Will ask again in the morning before we leave.

Saturday, May 15, 1954 morning

Went walking again last night—tried to find a place with music, but no luck. Found a good place to eat, though—had good omelet with lots of mushrooms. I had heard of a dessert made only in this section, so we ordered it. It is called Salzburg Nockerl. Jim was ordering cheese—but the waiter said the dessert was plenty for two—and he sure was right. It looked like a baked Alaska for 6 when he brought it in. I am still trying to figure it out—it was like the meringue on a pie, browned, but there was more to it—as though a thin custard had been added. Anyway it was deelightful.

I will be glad to leave here today. There is a most unfriendly attitude here toward Americans. An Army man had said there was—they don't like us and make no bones about it. They are simply out to take us—and if you don't like it—get out. The hotel employees are unbelievable rude, although this is the best hotel. They put extras on your bills and claim you had things—then they short-change you.

The money here drives you crazy. They have shillings worth $.04 and groschen worth 1/100 of a shilling! You have hundreds of dollars and they buy another, as prices are high.

Money is a headache anyway—first, in Ireland, we had pounds and shillings. In England the same thing, but English coins (they will not accept Irish coins). Then in Belgium we had francs. In Germany, marks and penning—and now this stuff! One shilling ($.04) is a coin the size of our quarter—but light like aluminum. Also, in change, you get handfuls of groschen.

Sunday, May 16, 1954 evening
Feldkirch

It would take a book to write about our trip yesterday from Innsbruck to Feldkirch. From the time we left we began to climb, until there was snow below us. The scenery cannot be described—you must see it to believe it. It was warm—still we passed cars with skis. When we got up very high there were sheds built out from the mountain over the trains—so the snow can slide over the tracks. We were just hanging on the edge—made you feel queer to see how little was holding us. We went through a great number of tunnels but one was a dandy—7 miles long! The work they have done is utterly marvelous. We passed the place where, in January, an avalanche took a train, plus tress, houses, etc. The rubble is still there. We crossed the divide—one side has water flowing to the Black Sea—the other to the Atlantic. Within the past year, a power plant has been opened which is another marvel! The plant is completely inside a mountain, and they use the water (melted snow), which comes down in torrents to furnish the power. Talk about the Seven Wonders of the World! They are out of date! The conductor spoke some English and he spent most of his time explaining things to us. We had a section to ourselves and he was very nice. It means so much when you understand things.

This is a small town and we came just for atmosphere—you really get a picture of the ordinary people. After the usual heaving of bags out the window we came to this small town hotel, which seems to be the center of social activity. There is a nice garden with tables and it is full most of the time—families eating and drinking. There are some characters! This afternoon a very large, poorly dressed woman came alone, and got a big glass of beer. She opened a bag and took out chunks of bread, then sat for hours, (about three!), with one glass of beer, just having her Sunday outing, eating and drinking. In the garden there is an enormous fish tank, full of speckled trout. When they get an order, the boy comes out with a net and gets them. Since we are steady, we get a linen napkin, which, at the end of the meal, is placed in a fancy envelope with our room number of it. Like having a napkin ring! Everyone in Europe has a garden instead of a lawn—flowers around the edge and vegetables the rest of the way. Today we saw the Austrian substitute for a scarecrow—where there is anything the birds might like they have a stick at an angle. Hanging from the end, by a string, is a small potato—stuck with long tail feathers from a chicken. It stirs and swings in the breeze, scaring away the birds.

There is something going on, in regard to the new school—so there was a parade, with band, yesterday. Today there was a special mass at the big church, with people in old costumes, etc. Then they went, behind the band, to the school. There were several hundred in the parade.

There is a large, rapid river through the town. They have walled it, with rock walls about ten feet high. On these, moss and flowers have taken root, so that entire sections are covered with flowers. They have bridges, but also catwalks to connect buildings.

I went to Mass across the street in a chapel of the Monastery of Capuchin (hope that's right!) monks. They wear brown habits and long beards. It is a beautiful chapel and today it has hundreds of white and pink primroses, arranged according to color.

Switzerland tomorrow!

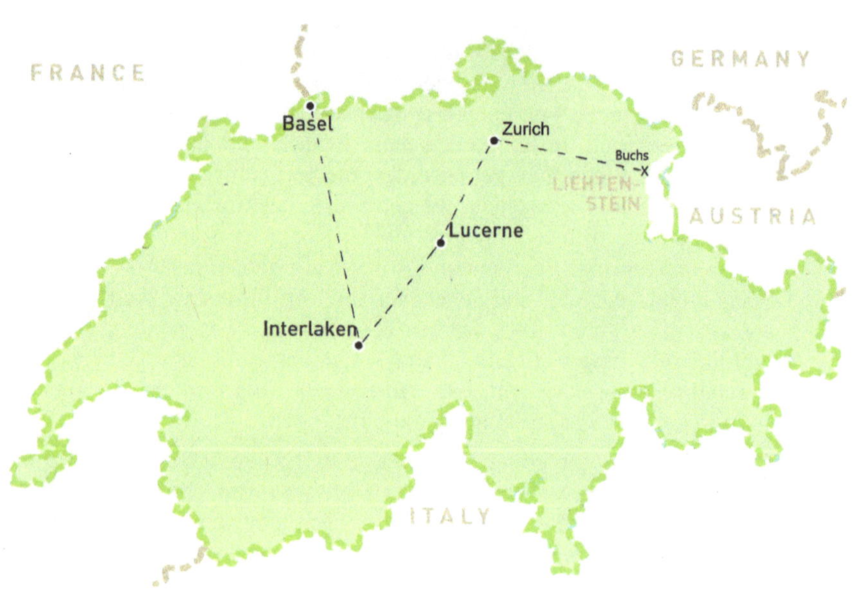

Destinations in Switzerland

Switzerland

Monday, May 17, 1954
Zurich

Well, another red-letter day for mail!! We left Feldkirch, Austria, this morning, after a nice weekend. So far as the trip here is concerned, I am running out of adjectives. The first part of the trip was the usual routine of crossing the border—two Austrians and one Swiss checked our passport. We crossed at Buchs, (in case you check the map). Then we got into some very high mountains with waterfalls every little way. It was just a sight. Soon we came to the end of Lac Zurich—and the rest of the trip we had the very blue water, with sheer walls of rock going up from it. We certainly came at the best time of the year, as the entire country is in bloom. All the orchards and flowering trees and shrubs are ablaze of color—and they plant their flowers in beds of one color so it really shows. I hope some of my pictures will be good enough to give some idea of the colors. They have many things also that we do not have—for instance—chestnut trees with big clusters of bright pink instead of our white ones.

I got a break here, as the porter came aboard and I didn't have to hoist the grips out the window. I told him I wanted a taxi (one word they all know) but also I told him the name of a hotel someone had given us. We were VIP's then—got into a swanky car with driver in uniform etc., and were driven to the hotel—only to find it full because of a steel convention. They called another hotel and we went there in a cab, only to find it was on a hill and Jim would have two flights of stairs to get into the hotel. We asked the driver to take us to a hotel and he brought us to one of the most charming ones you could want. It is small, but very well furnished and the cleanest place I ever saw. From our windows (entire side of both rooms is glass) we look into a lovely garden with lots of flowers and trees—from there to the lake below. It is quite a spot—Hotel Bellaria. We have two single rooms, with one bath and extra washbasin—balcony all the way across—overlooking garden. The manager, a woman, got quite excited when we wrote Chicago. She has a brother in Oak Park, whose son must be some musician. He sings and plays piano—gave a concert in Kimball Hall at eleven—sings with the Apollo choir, etc. She had all the press clippings. The assistant manager, a man, speaks some English. When we got here we were practically broke, as we did not want to get more money in Austria. When we were ready to go down to Cook's, I wanted to cash a traveler's check—the man was out—she could not cash it—told me to go down town. I made her understand I did not have cab fare! So she gave me 40 francs—($10) to tide me over.

Tuesday, May 18, 1954

Didn't finish last night, so here goes: Went to Cook's and got MAIL—Betty's letter, three from JMF and one from Irish Shipping. As it looks now—we will sail June 4th or 5th from Cork (Cobh) to Montreal. There is a remote chance of another boat to the States—but nothing definite. Looks as though we will just get home in time to greet JMF.

It was wonderful to get the mail. It is hard, with no schedule, for anyone to know where to write. Nothing from PMC and Jim is annoyed.

Had a wonderful dinner here. Good soup (clear and the color of consommé—a wee bit thick,) risotto (veal, cheese, and something which seemed a cross between rice and noodles). It was superb! Also had a green salad, which tasted wonderful. In Germany we were warned not to eat greens (like Japan) and I really miss my lettuce. For dessert I had a custard with a touch of caramel. Betty and I had one some-place. This morning I ordered poached eggs—so what I got was boiled eggs in the shell. Many funny things like that have happened.

I got quite a thrill this morning—Jim has had difficulty about baths, as there are no showers. He would get on his knees and dabble. Finally I tried something Babe told me years ago—she would have a patient roll over—get onto knees—and then up. We got that done quite easily—as I would help him up and down. This morning I got Jim in the tub—and he was to call me when he wanted out. He called me—when I got there he was out, and as proud as could be. We had planned to stay here for a day or so, but it is raining so we can't see anything—so will go on to Lucerne.

Wednesday, May 19, 1954
Lucerne

Had a nice trip up here, but a bit of an anticlimax—as we came through a long tunnel—into a large valley which ran all the way here. Any other time I would have enjoyed it more—but the scenery has been so spectacular that this was not appreciated. Lucerne is a nice city on a very large lake. The town is very old, with narrow winding streets like the "Mystic Maze." It is still raining, so can't do much. Our hotel, the Carlton-Tivoli is very nice—right on the lake. Food is excellent, and they have several large public rooms with easy chairs etc., so it is comfortable even in the rain. Got Betty's letter of May 12th and one from Keefe. I'm happy to get letters and Jim felt better when he heard from 6110. He went down town alone yesterday, and came back wet and upset. He couldn't find Cook's—and walked and walked. He undressed and went to bed—said he sure wouldn't want to travel alone as he can't find anyone who understands. It seems strange, for I have no difficulty finding places.

Finally found a hotel with fast service on cleaning and laundry—most places take at least a week—and on cleaning some take three weeks. We will start from here clean. Some places I can wash OK but with this rain nothing would dry.

I walked this morning—even in the rain—and saw something, which amazed me. Now I think I have seen everything. There is a large, very beautiful church—surrounding it is a wall—covering about a block. Inside the wall is what looked, at first sight, like a covered walk about 10 feet wide, with lots of flowers. Imagine my surprise to find it the burial place of hundreds of people, apparently buried one over the other for many generations. The "walk" is a series of stone slabs the size of a coffin. They are so old that many inscriptions are worn away.

The inside of the wall is completely covered with plaques—giving names, dates, etc, and several generations are on one plaque. The many flowers were the ones placed on a "grave" as we do at home. It is really a sight.

There are some lovely shops with laces, handwork, woodcarving, etc., —but the prices are fantastic.

This country seems very prosperous with huge factories, good homes, fine cars, etc. I guess it has paid them well to stay neutral—no war debts etc.

Thursday, May 20, 1954
Lucerne

The sun is shining—so things look brighter this morning. We sat around the hotel until evening—then walked. I had done two jaunts before so I really got my exercise—reminded me of Mexico.

We had dinner at the Walden-Mann, down in the old part of town—nice place and very good food—but full of Americans! I didn't come this far to see them!

Their specialty is chateaubriand—fixed in a way JMF and I must try. The meat, cut very thick—is partly broiled (browned). Then some cognac is poured over it and burned. A hot sauce is waiting in another pan—a sauce of cream, catsup, mustard, Worcester sauce, salt and pepper. The meat is sliced and dunked in the hot sauce—by this time it is cooked! Of course, I do not know the proportions but we can experiment.

Friday, May 21, 1954 morning

Had quite a day yesterday—walked and window-shopped until lunchtime—went into a place on a side street and had a good lunch. Jim has meat, etc., but I had a new one, which would be wonderful for a simple party. It was cheese fondue, made very thin—served in a casserole over a burner—so it "bubbled" all the time. With it was a long, sharp tined fork, and heavy bread, broken into bites. You dunk each bite and it was super. You could use rye bread and cut it to look better if desired.

We went on a steamer at 2:00 and were gone until 6:30. There are dozens of boats, which carry the mail, express, etc., and all the people who live in small towns on the lake use it to commute. There were many strange characters, and it was interesting to watch people getting on and off. Picturesque villages, nestling at the foot of the grim, snow-covered mountains. In the villages, as everywhere we go, flowers are everywhere. I guess, on account of melting snow, they grow so large and full of blossoms.

Returned to the hotel and cleaned up—went to Stadtskeller for dinner and music. We enjoyed the crowd, simply packed in—we even shared a table. Music was good—some funny. When they stuck to Swiss it was good, but on account of "turistas" they played some old American. Jim had a special—five kinds of meat—kraut—potatoes. I had a special also; it was veal, cut very thin, folded over, with ham and cheese inside, whole thing breaded and cooked like a wiener schnitzel. Here they serve lots of lettuce and vegetables, which I enjoy. On my platter were potatoes, green beans, tomatoes (broiled,) and asparagus. I also had a lettuce salad. We won't get thin, here.

Excerpts from letter from Lucerne, May 19:

> "More and more I hope George gets to come to Europe. Distances are so small that you see so much in a short time, and the people in service really have a wonderful chance; even GI's and wives get to see most of Europe."

Saturday, May 22, 1954
Interlaken

Well, we arrived here after many Oh's and Ah's—we keep going higher until we were nearly in the clouds. In many places we could not see the mountaintops, clouds were hanging so low. With melting snow there were myriad of waterfalls—big and small—while the lower valleys were a carpet of pink and blue flowers. This is not the season for Interlaken—it is so cold that last night with my coat over my suit I was shivering. But it is worth it. We are in a beautiful hotel—the Victoria—and from our windows I can look down at an exquisite flower garden or I can look up at one of the very high mountains, with more snow than South Dakota the time Jimmy walked there! Even Jim says this is the greatest scenery so far. The main attraction here is the trip to Jung-frau by rail. The railway station is 11,333 feet. It is much too cold to go—there is nothing going on here until the middle of June. At lunch yesterday we were the only ones in the huge dining room.

It is still raining, so will try to get a couple of pictures and leave.

We had an experience last night—went to the Kursaal to a concert. The first part was an excellent orchestra and the feature was the Glasgow Police Department bagpipe band! There were thirty of them—all in full regalia and kilts, high fur hats, etc. They were very good, had some wonderful dancers, drummers, etc., besides the pipes. We got a kick out of hearing them in Switzerland.

Over here all the shops sell clocks and music boxes of all kinds, you could imagine. Last night we had a good laugh—Jim was reading an ad for a compact—we wondered what Betty would say if we brought her a compact which yodeled!

Destinations in France

France

Sunday, May 23, 1954
Aboard the train to France.

We left Interlaken yesterday and came to the town on the border—which is Basel, Basle, or Bale—according to your nationality. Came through valleys and tunnels so it was not very exciting. Their tunnels are amazing (and countless). The longest I know of is 21 K, another 20, etc. They just go through the mountains instead of over or around. Swiss do not think much of the French—in the "bahnhof", which here is the depot, French customs, etc., they will not accept a French coin.

Our hotel was about third rate and dinner about the same—a little contrast is good for us.

We are stopping at Chaumont tonight.

Monday, May 24, 1954
Paris

Well, the best laid plans, etc!!! We sure changed our plans—happily! We were both disgusted yesterday, at the start of our trip. The train was so dirty and crowded—six of us in a small compartment. I don't think the toilet room had been cleaned since it was built. At noon we went into the diner—dirty table, dishes with particles of someone else's meal, etc. Food is served from large platters, and spilled on the table, floor, etc. You were fortunate if you were not wearing it! In that part of France the houses were unpainted, dirty, etc. All kinds of litter and rubbish were everywhere—dirty rags hanging over windowsills, etc. Fields were neglected. We saw no cattle and the entire picture was uninviting. We had been warned not to come to Paris without a hotel reservation, but just decided we would take a chance, rather than stay at Chaumont. A woman I had met in Lucerne had given me the name of a hotel—so we got a cab and sure were lucky. It is a small hotel—but very well furnished—nearly all speak English, and we are most comfortable. As to the location—it is wonderful. I can't tell you, but will make a sketch.

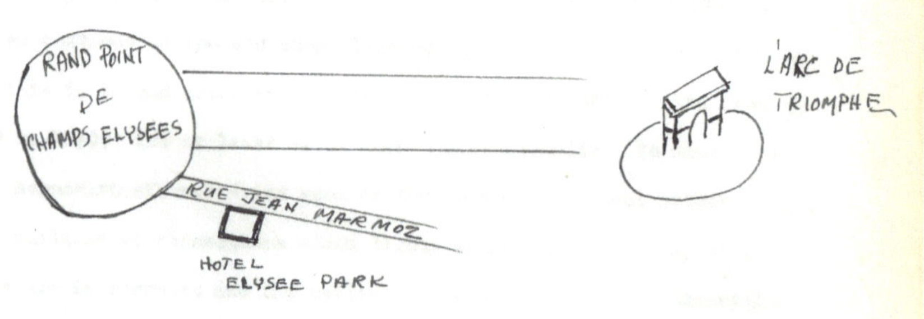

Location of our hotel in Paris

Got our mail this morning—two from JMF—one from Potter, and one from Irish Shipping. We are to sail from Dublin to Montreal unless something changes—arrive Montreal about June 17.

We walked the Champs Elysees last night—it is thronged with people and cars—very confusing, as it is very wide with cars and people trying to go in the same places. You think you are on a sidewalk until a horn makes you move—someone wants to park. In the center is 2-way traffic—then on each side two rows of parked cars—then more paving (and people walking,) then a single row of parked cars—then a wide sidewalk with countless shops and sidewalk cafes. We had drinks in a couple and food in another. Fun!

Today we walked some more and had lunch—also "did" Rue Royale." Tonight we are going to the Folies Bergere—isn't that something?

Tomorrow we take a Cook's tour—the only way for us to see a lot in a short time.

Tuesday, May 25, 1954

I'm a bit on the dopey side this morning—didn't get too much sleep. We saw the Folies Bergere! And what a show! I thought we saw costumes in the old shows like George White's Scandals, etc., but this is beyond description. There are about 40 acts (lasts from 8:30 to 12:00) and at least 30 of them are spectacular. So many acts have hoop skirt effects—and some of them must be ten feet across, with millions of rhinestones—and lights, which change colors, etc. The stage is enormous and the ceiling is so high they have wonderful stairway scenes with the gals coming down. In one act there is a pool—really water—deep enough to be over a man's head. Of course the bathing girls do not get wet—except the star—and she didn't have enough on to bother when she got wet. When we sat down, there was a mammoth birdcage suspended in the dome—I thought it was in lieu of a chandelier. Later the spotlight was turned on it—and there was a girl, sitting on the perch—they lowered it over the audience and she sang—then was pulled back up—the cage remained but I watched and she and the perch were raised through a hole in the ceiling. There was not much except music and dancing—so it really didn't bother us not to understand the language. It reminded me of going to shows in Mexico.

After the show we walked around the nightclub area—lighted like Broadway. We had something to eat, and so to bed. Excerpts from letters from Paris:

> "I can't believe yet that I am seeing all the places which, up to now, were just names...Tomorrow night we go to London (get on a sleeper here and wake up in London)...Now that the time is getting short, I am like a horse heading for the stable...Up to now, I like Bavaria and Switzerland. I am talking hard about Spain and Italy next. Guess I had better learn Spanish."
>
> "The AM, I was offered some obscene pictures by several. Almost had to call a gendarme to get rid of them."

Destinations in England

England

Thursday, May 27, 1954 morning
Crewe, England

Well, I missed writing yesterday—but have enough by now to fill a book. (!!!) Tuesday, we took a Cook's tour of Paris, which was fine. Instead of the usual "gabby guide" we had an elderly man, who really knew his business. Also, the trip we selected had no museums, so Jim enjoyed it. The two high spots were the Hall of Justice and Notre Dame. In the former, saw all the "barristers" in their robes and white jabots. The big shots who can plead cases before the high court also wear neckties. The building is, of course, very, very old, —was the residence of kings—the place where so many were beheaded. He sure gave us history.

Notre Dame is magnificent. Seats something like 25,0000 people. The windows are breath taking—three in particular which are high up and are round—each must be 30 or 40 feet in diameter. The colors are exquisite—so much light blue and lilac. During the war, they were taken down—piece-by-piece—and taken out of Paris to a very secret place. The outside of the church has hundreds of spires—most imposing. One strange feature is an arrangement of gargoyles—countless. The story is interesting—each carries off water from a section of roof—so on a rainy day the place looks like a huge fountain. But here is the significance: going to church you shed all your impurities—the gargoyles are symbolic.

We had a fine (and expensive) dinner at "Berkeley's"—after a couple of drinks on the sidewalk at Rand Point, a very popular spot. We took the boat train at 9:45, after the usual customs, etc. (French) Each time you cross a border you fill out a form for the country you are leaving and one for the country you are entering—names, addresses, when and where you were born (and why)—lots of red tape, but guess it is necessary.

We awoke in England, had breakfast, went through customs in London, and then the Day began. I guess we have been lucky—so we had to have one bad day. We had written for hotel—got there to find our letter came too late. We walked, rode cabs, busses, etc., for nearly four hours. Not a room to be had, the hotels kept getting worse and worse. I had called Mrs. Sullivan only to find she was very ill—so all our plans were shot. Finally I said we had better get out of London. Went back to Cook's where we had gone earlier to get some money. That was another headache—we had only a small amount of English money and we ran out! Cook's told us to go to Chester—nice town on our way to Dublin—train at 2:20. So we got our grips once more and drove to the station. No such train, but one at 2:20 going to Crewe, where we could stay and go on later. We were both tired and dirty after the night on the train—so we rode again until 5:30. Got here and asked for best hotel—right across the street—so porter escorted us. My face must have been a sight at what greeted us! The street is elevated—so we went down into a courtyard, which looked like you were going into a coal bin! The trains all have coal-burning engines—so everything is dirty. In the yard was a van, and dozens of old tables, dressers, wardrobes, etc. Inside the hotel, there was as much confusion. You may know how bushed we were when we still asked for a room. The girl explained that the entire hotel is being done over and according to law, they must remain open. I followed her upstairs, wondering if I could even sleep in such a place—we made our way through furniture, movers, carpenters, etc., to the end of the hall. She opened the door, and Behold! A room, new in every detail from carpet and furniture to a pale blue bathroom. If you think that wasn't relief, you are mistaken. After bathing and putting on clean clothes, we felt like new—and took a long walk. Slept late and have just had breakfast.

The hotel is huge—a block long and at least half a block deep. We had another surprise—at the back is practically a park—which covers about a full bock, and has lovely flowers, seats, etc. Since there are train sheds on both sides, they have trees and shrubs to cover them. It is rather startling to see the dirty front of the hotel, and then see the gardens.

Crewe is a large town—must be at least 50,000—but it is just a railroad center, without one decent cafe or shop. It looks about as clean and inviting as a coal town in Pennsylvania.

With all the difficulty—we could not get our mail—so Mrs. S is sending it to Dublin.

Trying to phone her was a major project—you go blocks to find a phone. There is a combination post-office, telegraph and telephone office—but not very frequent. The charge is 3 pence—copper coins about the size of a half-dollar. You deposit—lift receiver—and dial. If no answer—push button B for coin return. If they answer, push button A—otherwise you can hear them, but they can't hear you. All very complicated!

Friday, May 28, 1954 PM
Chester

Left Crewe at noon and came here—only 30 minute ride. This is the capital of Cheshire and quite a nice place. We were lucky to get a room—she apologized for only having room with bath! Room is not made up—American honeymooners just left and the place is full of confetti, etc.; however, they left a nice bouquet of lilies of the valley!

One of the strange customs in all hotels over on this side of the Atlantic is the stress on uniforms. All porters wear colored, long-tailed coats with lots of gold braid etc. Headwaiters all wear long-tailed coats, white tie, etc. In the hotel of last night in all the confusion the formal attire certainly looked out of place.

Plumbing here is old fashioned with water box for toilet overhead, with chain. The box is marked in large letters:

ROYAL DOULTON!!!

Destinations in Ireland

Back to Ireland

Saturday, May 29, 1954
Dublin

I am sure behind on my writing—so here goes for two days!

Our stay in Chester was wonderful—more than made up for London, etc. Chester is a perfect example of what my idea had been of an English village. It is very old—the old Roman wall still surrounds the main part of the city. The buildings are quaint and picturesque. Signs are priceless. For instance—"Ye Olde Bear's Head," "The Old Nag," etc. The houses are all so well kept, and big or little, they have flowers in every nook and corner. We did a lot of walking, and then took a boat ride on the River Dee. After leaving the town, where we passed the lovely homes on the riverbanks, the river meanders through beautiful countryside with an occasional castle or lovely home. Trees and shrubs line the banks—and they were all in bloom so it was one long parkway. We ate lunch in the hotel—very good—at night we ate in a "buttery"—strange place, which goes back to the time of Queen Victoria. Next morning, after breakfast, I joined the crowd on the sidewalk and got a close-up of Princess Margaret—who was to inspect the troops. Had hoped for a picture—but due to weather she was in a closed car.

We left Chester at 1:30 and went to Holyhead to get the boat for Dublin. We went early to see the town, which was a complete loss. It is just a seaport, nothing of any interest, except an old church, 1660. One thing I missed on the start of my notes was the fact that Holyhead is a port in Wales—so, by train, we crossed that small country, which, like Scotland, is governed by Great Britain. They have a strange language—and words, which must have thirty letters.

In Holyhead, after checking baggage, getting cabin, etc., we looked, in vain, for a place where we could eat. They were all so dirty we could not go in. Jim bought some tobacco—asked the young man for a place to eat. As a result, we took a bus—to the town a few miles east—where there was quite a good hotel. The ride was pleasant, as that is pretty country—half meadows and half the Irish Sea. We returned about 9:00, and went aboard the Hibernia, though it did not sail until 3:00. We had a good cabin, with bowl and toilet—so we were very comfortable. We were lucky to get a cabin, as some people sat up all night, or slept in a bin room with 40 bunks—one room for men, one for women. Took the train from boat to Dublin—only a few minutes' ride. Went first to Cook's for mail, and were lucky—had a handful. Then to Irish Shipping to check our boat. We are at the Russell Hotel—very nice small hotel across from "Stephen's Green," a small park.

Saw a mural in a post-office which I enjoyed—showed mail going into boxes—then to post-office—then by rail, truck, boat, plane, ski, motorcycle and donkey—to the postman who was putting it into an outstretched hand. Very well done.

Wednesday June 2, 1954

I have surely gone sour on the notes—nothing for days but there has been very little of interest—Dublin hasn't changed since we left—and I found it uninteresting before.

We gathered all our belongings into the Russell Hotel and I unpacked and repacked—which is a job I hate. We have more baggage than we had when we started—a great deal of stuff, which needs burning, etc. Jim asked me to make a scrapbook—and has one entire grip of stuff he has collected—most of which will go in the ocean. Monday we checked again with Irish Shipping and got permission to put part of our stuff on board. Jim had decided he didn't like the hotel—so simply loaded everything into a cab and started out—with no place in particular to go. We went to the Irish Oak and got rid of part of the grips—then started driving down the coast. In desperation I suggested a place we had eaten dinner before we went out of Ireland. So here we are. The hotel is small but clean and nicely located on the Sea. I had a miserable cold—felt like one of my sessions coming on—so went to bed early—took all kinds of dope and stayed in bed until Tuesday afternoon. Took a walk around the village and went to bed again. Felt better by this morning—so took a bus into Dublin—did some errands and some last minute shopping. Came back and rested a bit and then went on down the coast to the next village—Dalkey. I had been asked to call on some people there— which I did—but sure got my exercise. They live on the coast—a mile from transportation—but I didn't know that—so I walked—up and down steep hills—on rocks, etc, and me in very high heels! They lived in the US— Seattle—for several years—are very lonely and unhappy here—and seemed so glad to see someone from the States. I was glad I had made the effort. I figure I walked about 5 1/2 miles today—so sure am weary. I hope we sail on Saturday—now we are just killing time, I am anxious to get going.

Saturday, June 5th, 1954

Well—here we are—with our boat having labor trouble—long holiday—and no chance of sailing until Tuesday.

This is such an anti-climax—to just sit—that I am not enjoying it—to say the least.

Everything has seemed to go sour all at once, my cold—change of plans, etc. To really make a mess—we came to this resort on the sea—the weather went bad—and if there is anything more deadly than a resort in the cold, I don't know what it is. Since I am in such a stinky mood—everything bothers me—such as the foghorns, which blow every few seconds, and sound as mournful as a lost soul.

There must be a good reason for all this—but at the moment I can't imagine what it can be.

We rode the bus to Dublin yesterday—Jim finally saw the home of "Guinness Stout"—and we visited a beautiful church.

Sunday, June 6, 1954

We had a bit of a break in the monotony yesterday—went to the races. The headwaiter told Jim about them—so out we went, though we were a bit late. There were only six races—and two were over—but we had fun watching things. We were not in the clubhouse—just out with poor folks—it cost two shillings ($.28) to get in! There was one window where you could bet a pound ($2.80) but most of the windows and bets were two shillings. Also there were 12 to 15 bookies—all very busy—making their own odds and bets.

People got just as excited over their 2 shilling bets as they do at home on $2. We were lucky—had two winners in four races—one paid 3.50 and the other 7.50—so we did all right.

We had planned to go into Dublin for dinner, but were too tired!

Went to Mass at 8:00 this morning—and have not been out of the hotel since, as it has poured rain all day.

Tomorrow, Whit Monday, is a holiday and we will go to the races again—weather permitting. The jockey who rode our winner sat next to us at dinner last night—headwaiter introduced us—and he thinks his horses have a good chance tomorrow. He rides horses owned by a woman and they are all named—“Slipper.” The one yesterday was Irish Slipper—and he rides two others tomorrow.

Travel Home

Wednesday, June 16, 1954

Well, I sure fell by the way on the writing.

Whit Monday—Jim was sick with a cold—so we didn't make the races. Went to Jammets for farewell dinner.

Called Irish Shipping Tuesday morning—they said to be aboard by noon. So we did a dash—as we were out a long way. Then after our rush, we sailed at 4:00.

We are the only passengers—so have had a quiet time. We have two cabins with bath between and have been very comfortable. First day out was nice—then we left the Gulf Stream—so it was very cold.

Made good time for a while—so it looked as though we would get to Digby Wednesday. But—first we got into a bad storm. There was a blizzard in Newfoundland, etc. We had to slow down, it was so bad. Then when the sea was calm, Monday night, we ran into icebergs. We practically had to stop during the night, as they are not visible at night and are, or course, very dangerous. I saw one from my window and at a distance it looked like a boat. Today it turned so warm we sat out on the deck for a long time. Some contrast!

Word now is that we will reach Digby at 10:00 AM.

Jim has given up the idea of going on with them—would not be home for a couple of weeks.

I won't know until tomorrow about Betty and the car. I sent her a radiogram on Sunday that we would be in St. John Thursday. So tomorrow will tell! I'm very anxious to get going.

Men at table were very nice—Captain, Chief Engineer, and First Mate. No one else in the room.

Food good but strange. We ate breakfast at 8:00—coffee at 10:30—lunch at 12:00—tea at 3:30, dinner at 5:00—sandwiches, etc., at 8:30. No danger of starving.

Thursday, June 17, 1954

Arrived at Digby—the end of a pleasant trip—now only remains the trip to Amherstburg.

Friday, June 18, 1954
Montreal

Talked to Betty—plans were changed—so we took the train to Montreal from St. John, New Brunswick—having arrived there by ferry. Arrived Montreal in the morning—had a fine dinner at Desjardins. Leaving at 10:30.

Saturday, June 19, 1954
Amherstburg

Arrived at Windsor 1:55—taxi to Amherstburg—and, not the "song is ended"—but the book is done.

Part Two

Jimmy Flynn's South Seas Adventure & Other Musings

James Mitchell Flynn (2/12/1911–12/12/1963), better known by the family as "Jimmy" lived an interesting life. He traveled internationally, spending most of his adult years in Mexico, Canada and Greece. He began his international travel early. The story of his South Seas Adventure is his first independent, international travel.

Other writings include some of his letters written during this adventure and some short musings on friends and friendship. These writings share an insight into some of his thoughts. Time frames for the friendship writings and favored quotes are not identified.

A Little Background on the Merchant Marines

Ships and shipping in North America can be traced back at least as far as Leif Erikson. As the colonies grew, trade with Europe increased. Shipping provided the only conduit between the American colonies and Europe, and it continued to grow for almost two hundred years.

Merchant Marine Ships, owned by individuals and used for moving cargo could be called into military use depending upon the needs. Over the years conditions for those working on ships improved. The following laws implemented some of these changes:

1. The Seamen's Act of 1915. This act elevated public consciousness of safety at sea because of the Titanic sinking.
    - Abolished the practice of imprisoning seamen who deserted their ship;
    - Reduced penalties for disobedience;
    - Regulated working hours both at sea and in port;
    - Established minimum food quality standards;
    - Regulated wage payments;
    - Established specific levels of safety, ensuring availability of lifeboats;
    - Required a minimum percentage of seamen onboard to be qualified Able Seamen; and
    - Required at least 75% of seamen aboard the vessel to understand the language spoken by the officers.

2. The Jones Act of 1920 required U.S. flagged ships to be U.S. built, owned by U.S. citizens, 75% of the crew had to be U.S. citizens and only these ships could carry passengers or cargo between two or more U.S. ports.
3. The Merchant Marine Act of 1936. This was enacted to ensure there were adequate ships meeting the requirements of the Jones Act, which could serve as naval auxiliary in time of war or national emergency. The act also established federal subsidies for construction and operation of the merchant ships. Soon after this act passed, the U.S. Merchant Marine Cadet Corps was established and more structured training was required for those working on the ships.

The ship Jimmy traveled on was the SS Coldbrook, otherwise known as the SS Colebrook; a Hog Islander merchant ship that was grounded off Middleton Island, Alaska on 16 June 1942.

South Seas Adventure

James Mitchell Flynn (2/12/1911-12/12/1963), otherwise known as Jimmy was enjoying the holiday season when a telegram arrived at his father's office notifying Jimmy of his departure date on the SS Coldbrook. For those who understand little about seafaring life, Jimmy's story takes one on a maritime adventure to South America.

As an adult, Jimmy led an atypical life for his time. He owned property in Mexico City, Mexico; Montreal, Canada; and Greece splitting time between these locations.

1934-1935 The Trip

Working in the information department of the Century of Progress in Chicago in 1934, several of my fellow laborers and I formulated a plan to spend our last month's wage in traveling as far from Chicago as said wage would take us. We had in mind a trip to some rather tropical country, in the vicinity of Central America or perhaps Cuba. Truthfully, the plan was quite vague. However, I made mention of it at home now and then, with little or no parental comment. Consequently, it was a great surprise to me when father, on his return from a New York trip, told me that he had arranged for a trip down the East Coast of South America. It seems that he'd had some business dealings with Captain Michael J. Brennan, once skipper of Admiral Richard Byrd's ship on his original trip to the pole, and now Port Captain of the American Republics Line.

Through Captain Brennan, a place was to be made for me on one of the freighters plying its way up and down the Atlantic between Boston and Buenos Aires. Needless to say, I was excited at the prospect, and lost no time in spreading the news among my friends at the fair. But days lengthened into weeks and weeks into months, and I had not been notified to go to New York. Finally, the fair ended and the Christmas season approached, and with it the prospect of the family's annual trek to South Dakota, to spend the yuletide with my grandmother. By that time, I had practically given up all hopes of the ocean voyage, and, with the hustle and bustle of the holidays, I completely forgot it. Once more I was bowled over when, on the night of December twenty-sixth, a telegram came from Dad's Chicago office, saying word had finally come from New York, and I was to sail from Brooklyn Navy Yard at noon on December twenty-ninth. At first thought, it seemed out of the question, as we were 1700 miles from New York, with worse than poor rail service. As might have been expected, it was my mother who figured out that by driving something over 200 miles to catch a train, I could make the sailing.

We left Gregory, South Dakota, at ten o'clock that night, with Otto Ring, brother Jack, and my mother, arriving at Sioux City, Iowa at two a.m. The folks left me at the station at three-thirty, and I left there at five. I had a very uncomfortable ride to Missouri Valley, from which point I called John Keefe, Dad's secretary, the toll of $1.95 grieving me sorely. Also, I had to wait for more than an hour for the Chicago train. The trip into Chicago was miserable; arriving at 7:30, I went immediately to the I.A.C., for a bath and a shave. After a large dinner, I went out to get a railroad ticket, and then over to the Bismarck, where my alma mater was holding its Christmas dance. It was good to see a lot of the boys, and it was with reluctance that I left there at one, to return to the club and take to my bed. The excitement and anticipation found me awake long before the operator called me at 7:30, but I spent so much time breakfasting that I had to dash to catch the train at the La Salle Street station at nine. On the way through Fort Wayne, I wanted to call my friends, the Edwards, but had only found the number in the directory when the conductor shouted "All aboard!" I had never been East before and enjoyed the scenery through Indiana and Ohio; after dinner I read for a short time, but was well aware of the fact the next few days would be a strain, so was not too long in having the berth made up, and climbing into it.

I awakened someplace in New Jersey, and was soon in Hoboken, at the end of the line. I spent the next two hours on ferryboats and elevated trains, "lugging" my heavy bag to the American Republics Line dock, which I was later to know as Pier 34. I had been told to ask for Captain Brennan, so I did—for all of two minutes. He sent me aboard the ship, where I was given a bunk and saw the Boatswain. I had no equipment at all, so went ashore again to buy the necessities I was advised to have. When I returned, I was put to work, which unpleasant pastime lasted, with few all too short intermissions, until eight that evening. It was during that period of labor that I first learned the meaning of "red lead," for it was my job that day to rustproof numerous spots where some kind friend had chipped the paint in anticipation of my coming. I was much too busy to notice the motion of the ship after we sailed at four, although I did manage to steal a glance at "Liberty" and the Manhattan skyline. I learned a lot in a few hours, and all the fellows who made up the crew seemed to be all right. An unwieldy piece of cable "socked" me in the eye, but only bruised me. It was a wonder I wasn't killed, I was so clumsy. I found we were to go directly to Rio de Janeiro. The schedule was eighteen days, but several things were to delay us. The food, of which there was always plenty, tasted great after my first experience at manual labor. One of the other sailors had a radio, and I enjoyed listening to Paul Whitman for a short time before going to bed. There were eight of us in the forecastle, and the "bed" was none too comfortable, but it felt pretty fine to me. A word here on the term forecastle: On the SS Coldbrook, as in all modern ships, the word is really a misnomer, since it is in the stern of the vessel. It was, of course, originally in the bow, but during the last war, especially, with the ever-present danger of mines, the sailors' quarters were moved aft to lessen the danger in case of the explosion.

Sunday was just another day, though we did no work in the afternoon. It seemed that the usual routine was work, eat, and sleep, day after day. There was quite a sea running Sunday night, while we were crossing the famous Gulf Stream. It came up over the decks, and rolled the ship to the extent that we had to tie down the movables in the forecastle. Ordinarily, I'd have been unable to sleep, but I was so tired nothing affected me. Monday was just an aggravation! Everything the boatswain told me to do seemed more tiresome, and when five o'clock rolled around, I was ready to collapse. Then, at dinner, I was told to go up to the wheel from six till eight with Jim Lombardi, one of the able seamen. I lay down on the bunk for an hour, and then went up onto the bridge. Lombardi, whom I had liked from the start, was especially gracious and tolerant of my inability. As usual, the sea was rolling, and I had considerable trouble at first, but soon caught on to the tricks of the trade. We were steering almost due southeast; our course was set by the mate on watch and the compass number chalked up on a small blackboard before the wheel. We still heard excellent radio programs from the United States, several from Chicago, although the one most frequently heard was Atlanta. The boys had what were then considered tiny radios, but all of them were equipped for both long and short wave broadcast, and they tuned in European and South American stations with "the greatest of ease". The salt air had not yet begun to make me feel like a new man, but I had hopes. It was New Year's Eve, but I was in bed before nine, resolving to make up for the lost time a year later. (I did!)

Of course, New Year's Day was a holiday, which I certainly appreciated. We heard the Alabama-Stanford football game from the Rose Bowl at Pasadena, and enjoyed hearing the Southerners walk away with the game. I didn't stir out of my bunk that day except for the three meals. At that early hour I had found myself to be good sailor; at least, the "mal-de-mer" didn't keep me from eating.

Up next day at the usual hour of seven-thirty, and worked at soogee'ing the white paint which covers about a third of the ship. We worked, or so it seemed to me, furiously. Had several welcome recesses for coffee and cake, and quit at five. Strangely, I began to feel like myself again; felt fine all day, and ate like a horse. With Jim Lombardi as my tutor again, I took the wheel from six until eight. I had considerable difficulty getting on to the ringing of the bells, but soon had it down to Swiss perfection. The temperature when we left New York City was about forty, but had been rising steadily until it was quite warm. It rained frequently, though, and the showers, though very brief, were like ice. The radio programs that night were chiefly concerned with the details of the opening of the Hauptman trial. The fact I had only been a member of the ship's family of thirty for a few days didn't prevent my feelings that I was making substantial progress in establishing myself as a regular fellow.

There were eight of us quartered in the forecastle, as it was called. Along one side of the room were three double-decked bunks, while the opposite wall was occupied by one double-decker and several lockers. Here also were benches and lamps and radios and clotheslines and all the little personal possessions of these men of the sea. This room, perhaps fifteen by thirty feet in size, was home to these seven seamen and me. There we spent almost every moment not required by our jobs. It seemed quite impossible such a group could get along as congenially as they did. Of course, minor arguments arose from time to time, but there was never a fight during my three months aboard. What a different story from those I had read of the knock down and drag out battles in the lives of every sailor!

Another morning dawned, and now I was glad to see it come. That day I went on a regular watch. . . .From eight to twelve, reputedly a good one. On such a shift, I was to work from eight to ten in the morning, and then take the wheel until noon. After lunch, I was free until eight in the evening, at which time I took the wheel until ten, and then went on lookout until midnight. I was plenty tired that first night, and decided the romance of the sea might be a treat on the Nourmahal or the Corsair, but definitely not as an ordinary seaman on the SS Coldbrook. But there were many amusing moments, which helped a lot. The weather grew warmer daily, and the scenery of the sea, though rather monotonous, at time presented vistas unrivaled by anything ashore. The sunsets, flaming and golden, were truly beautiful, and at night the stars seemed to be within easy reach of my fingertips.

These things of beauty were forgotten completely the new day, for during the day I had to chip rust and paint with a pneumatic chisel. The pounding of the tools on these hot steel plates was deafening, and before the working day was over I was sure my head was splitting in two. However, during the period on lookout at night, from eight to ten, and following that, while at the wheel from ten until midnight, the third mate Mr. Perry carried on a rather one sided conversation with me. I was fascinated with his words concerning stars, and English cooking, and ships' engines, and was actually sorry when it was time to go to bed. We were to become close friends, and carry on a correspondence through many years. Mr. Perry, though born in Kentucky, had been in England most of his life, and had acquired the tea habit. Consequently, it was one of my duties to brew a pot of Lipton's for him each night at ten. And pleasant it was, for I took advantage of the chance to refresh myself, too.

On the following day, profiting by experience with air hammers, I obtained some cotton from the boatswain, and plugged my ears. As a consequence, I had no trouble at all, but, on the contrary, felt like a million all day. The weather had become so warm everyone lay about on the open deck either completely stripped or perhaps wearing an old pair of dungarees cut down to shorts. It was little wonder that the temperature was rising, since I was informed by my new friend, Mr. Perry, we were then directly opposite Miami, probably a thousand miles off the coast.

One of the amusing incidents of which I have spoken, occurred that day, illustrating one type of individual I met. Phil Gelski, nicknamed "Pollock," presented the theory the Unites States had given up the gold standard in order that the Lindbergh ransom money might be more easily detected!! Which reminds me to note here we received a daily paper of sorts. "Sparks," the radio operator, received the news over his powerful short wave equipment, and typed several copies of the more important events, which were then distributed over the ship. At that time, the Lindbergh-Hauptman case occupied most of the space.

The time seemed to pass more rapidly every day, and I was really and truly enjoying myself. My watch partner at the time was a wrinkled old salt, Andy Martin, originally from Baldholm, Sweden, and though others seemed to have trouble with him, to me he was both helpful and entertaining. My eight-to-twelve watch became a great pleasure, especially the afternoons that I lay in the sun. (About that time, I began to skip a day or more in my record of the trip.)

Mr. Perry entertained me by the hour with his fascinating experiences, and I found a vivid imagination was a great help at sea. For instance, any of my work became more pleasant if I imagined I was aboard my own yacht and merely doing my share. Sunday was so peaceful that the Coldbrook might well have been a yacht. We all thoroughly relaxed, the whole day through, spent part of the time on deck, part in the forecastle. (At the outset, I was bewildered by the fact that rooms in both the bow and stern of the ship were known as forecastles, but learned that the sailors' living quarters were originally forward, where many of them were killed during the last war when mines were struck. As a consequence, the sailors' room, the forecastle, has been moved to the stern of the ship, but retains its age-old name.) We carried our mattresses to the deck afternoons, and slept in the sun. Of course, I burned at first, but it was such a pleasant novelty for the first week in January I didn't mind at all!!

Boatswain Lloyd Thompson, Charlie Newton, and I often played cards in the evening; bridge when we were able to round up a fourth, otherwise rummy. I may have mentioned it before, or may later, but I must say here that I was somewhat amazed aboard ship to find the popular games—contact bridge, chess, and backgammon, (or as seafaring men over the world call it, "acey-deucy").

At that time, we were nearing the equator, and the sun was becoming increasingly hot. However, at sea, there was usually a comparatively cool breeze, and we were seldom uncomfortable. On the metal decks, the temperature often reached 120 degrees in the middle of the day, but in the shade it remained closer to ninety. At any rate, it seemed very cool for what was supposed to be the tropics.

The food on the Coldbrook was surprisingly good, far exceeding my expectations. We had cereal and eggs every morning, often with some variety of meat, with an occasional treat of fresh rolls and jelly. At noon we always had meat, potatoes, vegetables, and dessert, with a repetition of that for the evening meal, served daily at five, (to accommodate men from the various watches.) The cook, by the way, was a Chicagoan, and had spent most of his days on the Great Lakes, but enjoyed a southern trip every winter, if possible.

One of my most interesting acquaintances was Paddy Reynolds: his real name was John, but was known to all by his Gaelic nickname. We felt a common bond, since he had once made his home in Kilrush, County Clare, in Ireland, directly across the famous river Shannon from Tralee, in County Kerry, my grandfather's home. Nearly every day was brightened by this Irishman's colorful stories of Ireland and the world. Apparently there was no place on the globe, which he had failed to visit in his twenty-eight years at sea.

About that time, at the boatswain's orders, I gave up splitting the morning between the wheel and regular jobs on deck, perhaps because I was unhandy, and apt to let a pneumatic chisel go sailing over the side. And it was good news to my ears to hear henceforth I would spend my morning watch at the wheel. Those four hours were hell for the old timers, but for me they passed altogether too rapidly. Among other things I enjoyed were the flying fish, strange creatures about the size of a small perch, but having a curious wing-fin device on each side. They are able to fly until the wing-fin becomes dry, at which time they drop back into the water. (Boatswain Thompson lent me his copy of the Van Loon's geography, from which I learned much.)

My new job as "quartermaster" enabled me to remain much cleaner, a desirable condition on a ship where the only shower was salt water, and baths had to be taken from a pail. Nevertheless, regardless of occupation, we all took numerous baths daily, principally because it was a cooling and refreshing process, and the days were becoming terrifically hot. And the baths from a pail weren't bad. We filled it from a fresh water tap, and then put a pipe containing live steam into the water until the desired temperature was reached, and took a very splashy sponge bath. When one need not consider the clean bathroom, or the water, which may leak into the dining room below, a very satisfactory bath is a possibility.

As we approached the equator, the sun beat down upon the Coldbrook unmercifully. Even the nights became frightful. On deck, there was a semblance of a breeze, but in the forecastle, sleep was out of the question. It became a choice between suffocating inside in a bunk, or trying to sleep on steel or wood outside. And when we did sleep outside, notwithstanding the awning stretched over the entire poop, the sudden equatorial rains often drove us back into the stuffy but dry bunks.

A day or two prior to crossing the equator, the older sailors began to talk of some sort of hazing for me, something to which I actually looked forward. However, to my sorrow, the Neptune party failed to materialize. We played bridge almost nightly and spent much time listening to various radios. Reception as far as the states had become impossible, with the exception of powerful KDKA in Pittsburgh, but London, Paris, Berlin, and other foreign stations came in strong, all of them featuring American news, particularly the Lindbergh-Hauptman case. There were ten radios aboard, and the air above the deck resembled the roof of a metropolitan apartment building, with its web of antennae.

We crossed the equator at eight thirty-five in the evening on January eleventh, nineteen thirty-five.

Next day, Sunday, while playing hearts with some of the gang, a school of porpoises was sighted—about a dozen of them. They play a sort of "follow the leader" game at the bow of the ship and elsewhere, often-leaping clear of the water, one after another. The mate told me they are quite common in those waters, and I was to see many more of them, but have never forgotten that first school.

The temperature at noon the next day was an even hundred in the shade of my awning on the bridge, while in the engine room it varied between 125 and 145. Needless to say, I was very happy to be up top. Many of the fellows became more or less lethargic, to the point some of them only shaved once a week, some not at all until we arrived in Rio. (I felt much cooler and cleaner shaved, so didn't let the whiskers have their way for more than thirty-six hours.) The time spent at the wheel seemed to fly away, especially at night, for then the three of us, Andy Martin, Mr. Perry, and I carried on a three-cornered conversation on the bridge. In fact, all the time seemed to be flying by; it seemed impossible the trip was a fourth gone. But the daily routine and the many interesting incidents removed any and all traces of monotony.

Dad's birthday was the eighteenth of January, and I managed to send him a radio greeting, which I learned months later was more welcome than I had realized, for he was alone at the Illinois Athletic Club, suffering from a severe cold, when he received the radiogram. He was so pleased with it he had to exhibit it, and in the process forgot the cold and felt much improved!

January nineteenth of that year I shall never forget. On that day we arrived in Rio de Janeiro. Coming into the harbor was a truly beautiful sight. My vocabulary doesn't contain words to adequately describe it, but the famous "Sugar Loaf," jutting from the water to the sky, and "Corquevada," the 150 foot marble statue of Christ atop a thousand foot mountain, all framed in an abundance of the greenest grass, hundreds of steely royal palms, and the intense blue of the sea, proceeded such a scene of natural grandeur it brought a lump to my throat and tears to my eyes. The hour spent on the way to the dock in Rio made the entire trip worthwhile.

That first night, after being at sea for twenty-one days, I went ashore with Charlie Newton and Lloyd Thompson, the boatswain. We had several refreshing Tom Collins, and a delicious dinner, during which for the first time I had the world's most delectable cut of beef, the "Chateaubriand." I bought a few souvenirs, and some postal cards, after which we started a tour of the city. Rio's "red light" district is reputedly the most amazing in the world, and it certainly lived up to its reputation as far as I was concerned. It was, up to that time, at least, the most incredible hour in my life. There must have been literally thousands of girls, of every race and color, beckoning to the passing men from the open facades of their tiny individual brothels. Actually blocks and blocks of them, with an ample patronage!

We walked about and rode about in the open taxis for several hours, seeing the world famous mosaic side-walks, and many beautiful hotels and restaurants, frequently pausing at one of the sidewalk cafes for another drink or perhaps merely for some ice cream, which, strangely enough, all of us were craving. However, I must admit the gin bucks had a slight edge as far as popularity was concerned. I began to understand why sailors have the reputation of getting "falling down" drunk when they arrive at a port. They do need relaxation from the routine existence aboard a small ship, and liquor is one way for them to get it. However, I finished up the night drinking a quart of rather unpalatable milk. I had really missed that beverage on the trip, since we had, of course, nothing but canned milk. However, the milk in Rio wasn't what I wanted either, and I was somewhat apprehensive when it was brought to the table in what appeared to be a none too clean wine bottle! (The only place in South American I had the milk I was accustomed to was at Leo's Nacional Bar in Santos, for which I shall also remember plum ice cream and a salad made from palm hearts and the tiniest shrimp I've seen.)

In Rio I found many English speaking people, so it was not difficult getting about in the cafes and shops. Nevertheless, there was a distinctly foreign atmosphere prevalent. On the other hand, the architecture of office and apartment buildings was much more extremely modern than anything I had seen in the states, and the streets were teeming with American cars, principally Fords and, as taxis, many decrepit Buicks and Packards.

During the day all the time we stayed in Rio I had the job of standing watch in one of the holds in the bowels of the ship, watching the eminently dishonest stevedores handling cargo, to make sure they did not steal all of it. (When handling sugar, they often are known to break open a bag, fill all their pockets, and leave without being detected.) A great many of these notes were written while I sat upon a bag of sugar or crate of Mobil oil, with one eye on a stark naked Brazilian, the other on my paper. A curious law over all of South America makes it imperative that all men wear coats everyplace; one may not board a streetcar without a coat. The stevedores come to the docks dressed neatly, but when ready to go to work, fold every stitch and lay the bundle aside until time to go home.

We stayed in Rio but a few days, since it is primarily a resort, and actually not much of a business center. From there we proceeded to Santos, only a short run down the coast, where I found an extremely interesting city, thriving with business. Santos is reputedly the world's largest coffee port, and it would seem to be true. The docks there have been designed to handle coffee, and it is fascinating to watch them load the ship. Huge conveyors, similar to those used for handling bananas in New Orleans, are rolled alongside, and a long arm extended toward the center of the ship. The bags of coffee are brought along on endless belts to a series of smooth, wide planks leading to the hold itself. The workers are all in the bottom of the hold, and as the first bags come down, they are built into a sort of pyramid. After that, their job consists mainly of guiding the sacks as they come sliding down the side of the heap.

Santos is situated on an island, and tall mountains rise seemingly all about it. The buildings, as in Rio, are most interesting that the newer are pages are from the Architectural Forum, while the older shop buildings carry out the common tropical idea of having a front like a large roll top desk. When they are ready to close for the night, the roller comes down, is locked and the proprietor goes home. This enables them to have more light and air, and flies!

We docked in Santos about five in the afternoon, on a Sunday; before arriving there, several of us had spoken of taking a run up to Sao Paulo, but we were so late it was out of the question. Lloyd Thompson, the boatswain, had asked me to have dinner with him, so I bathed and dressed in my best. We went directly to Leo's Nacional Bar, one of the finest places to eat or drink I have seen anyplace. Leo is an ex-speakeasy owner, although a native Portuguese-Brazilian, and knows how to attract and satisfy the public. He has immense glass refrigerators all about, filled with delectable roast fowl, rare old cheese, everything to make ones mouth water. Thompson and I sat down and had a grand dinner, with the usual steak, although of course I ordered another "Chateaubriand." Captain Story, our skipper and Dan Sterns, the assistant engineer were at the next table, and asked us to join them after dinner. Thompson accepted and began a most enjoyable incident. After a few drinks, Sterns, a fine chap from New York, excused himself, having some "unfinished business" to take care of. Almost as soon as he left, the skipper turned to me and asked if I would care to see some of the sights available in Santos, warning me that I must keep the experience to myself, since it was, of course, extraordinary for the Captain of a ship to entertain one of his ordinary seamen. I accepted with alacrity assuring him of my intention to say nothing about anything.

We left Leo's and started a tour of the lesser spots, missing very few of them. Then, at about midnight, Story hailed one of the "fresh air taxicabs," in which, at his direction, we were driven off the island to the foot of one of the towering mountains, to the station of an inclined railway. Tickets were purchased, and we were soon on the way up, up, up.

We climbed what I afterward learned was something over a thousand feet, to come upon one of the most amazing sights possible. Atop Monte Serrat is the Monte Serrat Casino, a magnificent building three stories high, with elaborate rooms for gambling, dancing and dining. The skipper was well known there, and we were soon seated at a table on the edge of the large dance floor, while two orchestras alternated in entertaining the crowd. And what a crowd! It was unbelievable that in, or near, this spiggoty town in Brazil could exist this beautiful showplace, thronged with the most smartly dressed men and women, champagne flowing like water, a scene out of Paramount! I was brought back to reality by the appearance of three of the many hostesses coming to the table, all-Spanish or Portuguese speaking, while I was unable to do more than smile happily! We danced if it can be called that; they wanted to tango and rumba. I didn't know how. They wanted to teach me. I didn't know the language. For the first time, I believe, a man took dancing lesson by Braille! But it was thrilling, and even at four-thirty, I was loath to leave. We made a few more stops, and trudged aboard the ship as the sun rose over the Atlantic.

I had to work aboard the next day, that is, watch cargo, and the day was a beastly hot one. However, it boiled all the champagne out of my system, and that evening we contented ourselves with another meal at Leo's and a movie, fortunately an American production with Portuguese subtitles dubbed in.

In Rio Grande do Sul, the next port of call on the way South; I had a day to myself, so I wandered about the city all day, enjoying it a great deal. The country in that vicinity is largely agricultural, resembling some of our own Western country, grazing cattle, horses, sheep, but still more or less tropical, with the native trees and flowers. The docks were about two miles from the "city," which made the street car ride (by Brill, of Philadelphia), a pleasure, affording a fine view of the city with its hundreds of red and yellow tiled roofs. Saw an interesting native market, offering for sale everything from parsnips to parakeets. During the afternoon I came upon an old Catholic church, the cornerstone of which carried the date 1755. It was a gracious old building, beautiful in its very simplicity. Disappointing, however, was one feature of the interior: with exotic flowers blooming everyplace, the altars of this venerable edifice were decorated with artificial blooms, or wire and paper. Typical, though, for even in the parks, naturally lush, the hibiscus and orchid are relegated to some obscure spot and the common American sunflower takes the center of the stage.

From Rio Grande do Sul we traveled on southward to Montevideo, in Uruguay, where I regret to say we spent little more than a day and a half, working cargo practically every minute of the time. However, I did have time to see the downtown section of the city, and had "tea complete" in one of the veddy, veddy British tea emporiums. I discovered later we missed one of the small but frequent revolutions by a few hours. Perhaps it was just as well that we left when we did, but I'd like to have seen what a revolution looks like!!!

Montevideo was near the mouth of the Plata River, a broad and very muddy stream on the order of the Mississippi, but greater in size. At its actual mouth, it is some forty-five miles wide, and it is strange to see the water change in a few feet from the blue green of the sea to the brown of a muddy stream. Leaving Montevideo, we sailed up the Plate, as it's known in English, about a day to Buenos Aires, docking there on a Tuesday afternoon. I had planned to see some of the city yet that night, before something happened to defeat my noble intent. However, the headlines on the local papers read "HOTTEST DAY IN THE SEVENTY-EIGHT YEAR — OFFICIAL TEMP 108 DEGREES." The result was after I had bathed and dressed, I found it too, too simple to join some of my friends at the Ukraine Bar, the first one on the way from the docks to the city proper. It was delightful to sit on the terrace there drinking the excellent Quilmes beer, with the lights of the skyscraper office building and hotels twinkling a few blocks way, and it took fortitude to take leave of the company. But I had made up my mind to take a personal sightseeing tour on foot that evening, and after half a dozen beers managed to get started. I must say that I did walk for about two hours, and got a fair idea of the downtown part of the city. However, upon returning to the docks and Coldbrook, I discovered Perry and Sterns aboard, quaffing more Quilmes from a gallon bottle. I accepted their invitation and joined them, which of course finished the bottle in short order. I volunteered to go to the Ukraine for another, which was my mistake, for arriving there I found almost all of the crew from the skipper on down. Our gang had literally taken over the place, and I was asked to join them. The net result was I didn't get back with the gallon, but Perry and Sterns had to follow me! The latter part of that evening is somewhat hazy. I learned through the fog of a ghastly hangover the next day that at one point I felt the heat to the extent that I doffed my shirt and poured several steins of beer over my own head in an effort to "cool off". (What I did succeed in doing, I know, was to magically change what had been the hair of my head to a thriving crop of shredded wheat!!!)

We returned to the ship at dawn, and the following day found me too ill to so much as watch cargo. I struggled through the day, and that evening had an interesting but extremely mild time with, "Jonesy," one of the oilers, a young lad from Kentucky. We had a good dinner and went to the performance at the "Broadway" theatre. The bill consisted of a movie followed by two short plays on the stage, and lasted, in its entirety, from nine until one. We stuck it out until about midnight, at which time we strolled back to the docks, stopping en route for MILK and ICE CREAM!!!

On Thursday I puttered at many odd jobs under the direction of my friend the boatswain, and as soon as 5 o'clock rolled around, we all dressed and headed ashore again. Tommy (the boatswain), Charlie Newton, Jonesy, and I went first to the Floriday, or, more correctly, the Calle Florida, a smart and fashionable street which is closed to all vehicular traffic from four until eight daily, so the fashionable and unfashionable who wish to appear fashionable may promenade. The street is a succession of fine shops, tearooms, and elaborate bars, and about what would result if one took the best of Fifth Avenue or Michigan Boulevard and condensed them into a few blocks. We went first to the Boston Bar, supposed to be the most popular with Americans. It was a huge place, with a comfortable atmosphere very conducive to drinking. A good orchestra played light music from a balcony, while the customers sat in large armchairs in air-conditioned ease. Most of the patrons turned out to be either American or English, so it was a pleasant change from the many native places we had visited before.

After a pleasant hour or so at the Boston, eating and drinking (they plied us with trays of delectable hors d'oeuvres along with delicious drinks!), we strolled back to the Plaza de Mayo, and from there finally to the Munich Cafe on the Avenida de Mayo. The Munich, one of three fine restaurants bearing the same name, is as German as Berlin, with typical German waiters, and a small string orchestra playing someplace in the background. My companions had been there many time before, with the result that as we came in, in view of the fact they were from Kentucky, Georgia and Florida, the orchestra struck up a medley of Southern tunes. We had as marvelous a dinner there as I have ever eaten anyplace, accompanied by several bottles of an old Spanish wine, a perfect complement to the meal. The entree was, of course, beef; and what? Beef! We ordered tenderloin, but nowhere else have I seen such a cut. It was about the size of a salad plate, and more than an inch think. Food for the Gods!!!

We must have remained there for almost three hours, but finally found ourselves on the Avenida again. Someone suggested the Phoenix Bar. It turned out to be another typically English place, operated by a Mr. and Mrs. Fisher. Mrs. F. played the piano while the customers, nearly all of them "limeys", sang her songs. We stayed there for another two hours, and then headed back to the ship, making lengthy pauses at the Avon and Ukraine bars. Friday was almost a repetition of Thursday, except Tommy and I went to see a fair movie, had cocktails in a couple of new bars, and a delicious dinner at the world-famous Jousten Hotel. We ate and talked for almost four hours after which we followed our usual devious route to the ship, via the Avon and Ukraine bars. On Saturday, we had the afternoon off, but I spent most of it in the post office, getting off my many postal cards and airmail letters. I can recommend unconditionally the Buenos Aires post office for it offered the finest pen available, and an English speaking information attendant. I met Tommy and Elbert Jones at the Boston Bar once again, and after a few cocktails, we returned to the Munich Cafe, for our last B.A. dinner. I shall never expect to eat such a delicious dessert as the "Merengue Munich". We had planned to get to bed early, because we sailed the next morning but we met our Waterloo at the Ukraine, where we sat drinking "Caballo Blanco", or White Horse, as it's called at home, until the wee hours. I found the miniature ice bucket of silver was a fine stamp moistener; must remember that when I have many letters to mail again. Although it was nearly four when we retired, I arose at 6:30 and went to the magnificent Cathedral to mass, but I almost regretted going, for it took a week to convince the crew who saw me come aboard at ten a.m. that I hadn't been ashore all night.

We sailed at noon, going directly to Santos to load 20,000 bags of coffee, and 3,000 cases of corned beef. We had but one night there, and Charlie Newton, Jones and I went to the "Santos Paramount", where we saw a good movie and several rats. The next afternoon I was free, so I visited our friend Leo, at his Nacional Cafe, and had one of his exotic salads of baby shrimp and hearts of palm, swimming in mayonnaise, followed by several dishes of his equally fine plum ice cream and the nearest approach to the milk at home I was able to find. On Perry's advice, I purchased three quarts of Cognac, and a liter of Brazilian coffee. The coffee reached home all right; the cognac went the way of all cognac, in Para. I managed to salvage one bottle for my brother Charlie, that connoisseur!

Three weeks later! (2/26/1935) We sailed from Santos up around the "corner" to the little town of Ceara. There were no docks, and very little harbor — just a sort of cove. The cargo, mostly wax to be made into furniture polish, had to be brought out to us on barges. I was free in the afternoon, so I decided if I was to go swimming at all in South America, I had better do it while I had the chance. There were conflicting stories as to the presence or absence of sharks in the water, but I went in anyway. I must admit I didn't enjoy it a great deal, for the water was rough, and I had to dive over the side, a distance of nearly twenty-five feet. Fortunately, the gangway was down, or I'd have stayed in Ceara, for I couldn't get up a rope if my life depended on it, and a rope ladder was almost as bad. Not being allowed ashore in Ceara, there isn't much to say about it. However, it's an overnight stop for the Pan-American Airways, has a radio station and the buildings look modern. About half of them seemed, through the binoculars, to be churches. The only name I was able to see was one "STANDARD OIL". Leaving Ceara, we made a short run to a place called Tutoya. There was no town at all, only two thatched huts on the shore. And the only harbor was the natural one formed by the presence of a circle of sand bars.

The cargo, the stevedores, etcetera, must travel from the village of Parnahyba, 100 miles up a tiny river. The water was infested with sharks, barracuda, and some small fish (piranha) with a double set of razor sharp teeth, which are capable of eating a live pig in ten minutes. Naturally, no one thought of going in the water there.

The Sunday spent there happened to be my birthday (24th). I never expected to spend one of them amid stranger surroundings. Friend Perry toasted me with some fine Scotch, and the day passed pleasantly, if uneventfully. Saw a strange sight when the stevedores ate their meal aboard the ship. It consisted of fish, cassava meal, and a wild hog, made into a sort of ragout or stew. There were 40 of them huddled about the #3 hold, in the weird light of flares, eating off their home made plates of tin, using only their sheath knives and their hands as implements. Our next and last port was Para, 100 miles up the Amazon River. That city was probably the most North American city visited, but at the same time, the most tropical. Situated within five miles of the equator, it is completely surrounded by dense jungle. Over 150 varieties of wood are found within a few miles of Para, and as many types of wild animals. Saw numerous monkeys and snakes about the city. I picked up a young East Indian boy for a guide, and spent a pleasant afternoon wandering about the city. Went ashore in the evening with the intention of eating and returning, but we (Newton and I), ran into Perry and 2nd Mate Peterson, who insisted that we have a few drinks with them. Spent a very amusing evening, trying to understand the jargon of the native girls who infest every barroom. Some of them have their teeth filed, and still possess the fuzzy black hair so long associated with jungle people. The funniest sight is to see them smoke their big, black cigars. It has to be seen to be appreciated!

Everyone keeps away from actual contact with them though, for it is general information that about 85% of the natives of Brazil are diseased.

We left Para in a terrible rainstorm, and had only been at sea a few hours when we lost a blade off the propeller. We had been due in New York the first week in March, but had to cut our speed in half and thus lost a week. I was quartermaster, that is, I steered all the way home, and so it wasn't bad for me.

In conclusion, we loafed along at about four knots, all the way into New York; the office of the company had radioed Captain Story to use his own judgment in either putting into thru West Indies for repairs or gambling on fair weather to get us into New York. Of course, he took the latter course, and we made it. However, we did have some bad weather before tying up at Pier #34. At the time, there were severe storms all over the North Atlantic and several ships had gone down. Thus, it was with a sigh of relief, that we found the Coldbrook in her berth in the Atlantic Basin in Brooklyn.

She was put into dry dock there in New York, to my great pleasure, so that meant more time in Manhattan. Managed to see Captain Brennan for twenty of his valuable minutes and Jimmy Boylan for an equal period. Saw a lot of the city, both by myself and in the company of Tommy. We managed to get tickets for Grace George in "Personal Appearance," and a couple of nights later I obtained a single seat for "Life Begins at 8:40." In brief, I saw about all there was to see, from Riverside Drive to Wall Street; spent a lot of time in Times Square, and my middle western eyes missed very little.

The officers wanted me to stay on the ship for another trip, which was, to say the least, flattering to me. However, I was anxious to get back to

Illinois, and after an overnight trip up to Boston, and a few hours there as the guest of Jim Hurley, State Civil Service Commissioner, I was glad to entrain for home.

Arrived in Chicago, after nearly three months away, resolving already to see South American again. (I still have hopes!)

Letters to Family

Thursday, 1/17/1935

My dear family —

We are due to arrive in Rio at dawn tomorrow so I am writing this today as to get it in the first mail.

First of all, I am enjoying myself immensely, and doing very little actual work. For the first week I did quite a bit, but soon the boatswain, who is our boss, saw that I did less than the others because I knew less about it. Consequently, since then, I've spent nearly all of my time at the wheel. I am on the 8-12 watch, so that my hours are as regular as if I were at home. The food is fine, even better than usual according to the veterans. Weather has been well, nigh perfect. I had no chance to don heavy underwear and the highest we've had was 90 degrees.

The gang aboard here are for the most part OK. Most of them Southerners from Georgia, the Carolinas and Florida. One boy, Charles Newton, Waycross, Georgia — 23, blond 5'10" has been to college, but likes this life. We play bridge nightly, with the boatswain, and the 3rd mate often joins us. Spirit evidently entirely different from other officers I've met, very congenial.

3rd Mate and I talk all the 4 hours I am on watch at night.

Capt. Story is the skipper; fine fellow, though we hardly even speak to him.

I saw Captain Brennan for about 2 minutes the day I arrived in N.Y.C. He was busy and so was I. I haven't been seasick at all, and feel like a million. We had some rough weather but I came through like an old salt.

Rio is swell! More later!

There are ten radios on the ship, one in our forecastle. We hear programs from the states all the time, and get news reports several times daily. For instance, heard about the San Quentin prison break. Ottawa, Ill. bank robbery, and slaughter of the "Red" Banker family yesterday. Also had the Alabama Stanford game on New Year's Day. Lindbergh case reported every evening.

We are to be in Rio only for a day, but it should be sufficient for me to get an idea of the place and a souvenir or two. A crowd of us is planning a trip into the Brazilian interior from Santos to Sao Paulo, Sunday afternoon if the schedule works out OK. If not, we'll go swimming at the much-heralded fine beach in Santos. Seems a great pity to see all this clear blue water swishing by when I can't dive into it.

The trip is 1/4 over now and the next of it will pass quickly, for we'll be in and out of port a lot. As a whole, it's very enjoyable, but on the other hand, some of the life is only enjoyable as hitting ones head with a hammer. I'll be awfully happy to be home, and what's more, to settle down to a job if I can get one. Wish I were older, so that I could do something in the Potter Company.

I certainly miss all of you. I was never very homesick at school, but that was never more than 300 miles away. These thousands between us make me want to get home and stay forever.

I hope to hear from you in B.A., and if you answer this letter by airmail I'll get it OK. We expect to be back to N.Y.C., by March 10th, and what a happy day that'll be.

I'll put what I've forgotten here in another letter from the next port. All my love to all of you, hoping that you're well and happy.

—Jimmy

1/21/1935

My dear family —

I'm in a gambling house in Santos, the biggest coffee port in the world. Having a great time.

Rio was the most beautiful city I've ever seen. You must see it sometime; the fare down here isn't much — probably no more than the cost of a month in the South.

We went out the one night we were in Rio and had a grand time. Had about a half dozen Tom Collins, and then a marvelous dinner. From there we walked and taxied about the city from the exclusive "Corcovado" district to the red light district, comprising about half a mile square. Probably a thousand fallen women, all at their windows and doors. Never heard such a bedlam.

The harbor at Rio, with Sugarloaf and that statue of Christ was breathtaking. Even though some aspects of the trip have been a little tough the half hour spent coming into Rio harbor made it all worthwhile.

Santos here is an 18-hour run from Rio. Arrived Sunday afternoon, so went out to dinner at Leo's National Bar. (Leo used to operate a speakeasy in the U.S.A.) Had dinner with the boatswain; the Captain and 3rd assistant engineer were next to us. They asked us to join them, and we did Santos till 5 this morning. Visited the exclusive Casino atop Monte Serrat; fine orchestra, beautiful women in attractive gowns for hostesses and much champagne, all on the skipper. All in all, a swell night. Leave for Rio Grande de Sol tomorrow and from there to Montevideo and BA.

Drank martinis, gin fizzes, champagne and beer last night, but tonight it's ice cream. Everyone down here eats gallons of it, and it makes drinks look like Walgreens. I'm working on a dish of plum now. Try it sometime.

We're only staying in B.A., 4 days and are going to Para — 60 miles up the Amazon. Everyone likes a short stay in B.A., for it saves money, which it too easy to spend down here.

You can see I must close. More from Rio Grande de Sol. Write me at Santos at once.

Love, Jimmy.

Saturday, 2/2/1935

Dear family—

We've been here in Buenos Aires for five days and are sailing at eleven tomorrow morning. Have had a fine time, but it's all so wonderful that it seems a dream. We've had to work all day everyday, but the nights have been perfect. Food is the best I've ever eaten, and very cheap compared with the U.S.A. restaurants.

We're going from here to Santos in Brazil, where we spent a few days on the way down. From there we head for Para and several other small ports, and on to New York, arriving there, according to the new schedule about March fifth.

I was disappointed when I didn't hear from you here, but I can look at it from the standpoint of "no news is good news." Kind of tough though, after I've been so diligent about writing. Maybe there'll be something at Santos. I did have a letter from Virginia McKinzie from Miami, written on Jan 2. They're having a grand time too, and planning to be in New York about the time I get in.

I didn't get to see Cy Mulligan as I have nothing but Swift's address for him and they have always been closed before I could get to a telephone or down there.

We're all sorry to miss Sunday in town here, but it will save money for us, and heaven knows we spend too much of it here!

I have done no shopping at all, so I must dash downtown now, and scout around. I'll let you know from Para whether we're going to New York or Boston first, so that you can write me there.

I've rid myself of a bad cold, and feel fine now. Developing a beautiful coat of tan— Ginny and I are having a contest to see who has the browner back. 108 degrees officially here two days ago— hottest in 78 years.

Do write— please.

Love to all — Jimmy

2/17/1935

Dear Mom and all—

Arrived in Santos today, to take on 20,000 bags of coffee, leaving tomorrow afternoon. Weather clear, tracks fast, as usual.

I was pretty disappointed again today, when there was no letter waiting here. But now I'm more worried than anything else. I know that if you folks are as lonesome for me as I am for you, I'd have had mail either in B.A., or Santos. The natural conclusion for me to draw is that something is wrong. It's kind of tough to be away down here, thinking so often about home, but it's worse when I'm afraid something has happened to prevent you from writing. However, it won't be long till we will be back in New York (between March 2nd and 5th), and then I'll know. Feb 17th won't be very happy now.

We go from here to Ceara and Tutoya and then, up the Amazon to Para, then directly to N.Y.C. If they continue to knock off 300 miles a day, we may be home before March first.

I'm working pretty hard everyday now and it's hotter than the weekly $700, but I'm acquiring a beautiful coat of tan and the labor is doing me a world of good.

Please drop a line to Ginny McKinzie — 57 S.W., 6th St — Miami and tell her I'll be in the first week in March and if she and Bertha are in N.Y.C., I'll drive home with them if they'll let me share the expense.

It's much too hot and muggy to write more now. I pray that all is well. (Went to mass in B.A. Sunday — the only chance I've had!)

Hoping for the best, with love to everyone.

______ Jimmy

Tuesday, 2/19/1935 1:30 a.m.

Dear family —

This is probably my last letter from South America. We are due in Para tomorrow night at about 11:00, and weather permitting, in New York, March fourth. I must go on to Boston to be paid, but that will mean but two or three days more, and the time we stay in N.Y.C., will give me a chance to see the city without much cost.

I am hoping that either you or the McKenzie's will be in New York about the tenth of March when I will be back from Boston and ready to start for home.

Since leaving Santos, we have visited two unique ports if they can be dignified by that title. The first was "Ceara," which is nothing more than a small city set down between the jungle and the sea. There are no docks, so we anchor out a half a mile and the cargo is brought out on barges. The cargo, by the way, consists of goatskins, castor beans and wax. Notwithstanding the rumored sharks, I went for my first salt water swim. Wasn't in the water twenty minutes, but the dive off the side down to the water some twenty feet away and my surprising immunity to the disagreeable qualities of salt water made me quite a name, at least for the day. (You can judge that there are few swimmers in the crew!)

From Ceara to Tutoya, what a place! Nothing but a shallow bay surrounded by jungle. The town of Tutoya consists of three shacks. Again we anchor out, and the freight — more wax and castor beans — is brought more than 100 miles down a river. Spent Sunday, my birthday here, but no swimming, on account of the presence of numerous barracuda.

Mr. Perry saluted February 17th with me in several drinks of his excellent Scotch, and the day was pleasant, all in all. The 40 or so stevedores ate their single meal aboard at 8. Fish, pork, cassava meal, and rice, in a huge stew, heaped on old pieces of tin, eaten either with fingers or a sheath knife. What a sight for Emily Post!

Please let me know what is going on c/o S.S. Coldbrook American Republic Lines, Pier 34 Atlantic Basin, Brooklyn, N.Y., and prepare to kill the fatted calf about the twelfth of March.

I hope Charles still keeps my Xmas cards.

Much love to all.

/ Jimmy (Or, as I am called here, "Mike".)

Friendship #1 Writing

It seems to me one of the greatest purposes of life is to gain and keep a friend or two. I often wonder what any of us would do if we didn't have at least one friend, held in reserve, for the dark or discouraged hour.

Woodberry says of Wendell Phillips, who devoted his entire life to the betterment of humanity, that he had very few friends during the early part of his life, and at it's close he seemed a very lonely figure as he walked the streets of Boston. One day he came upon Nora Perry, the poetess, whom he knew very well. He asked her where she was going. Her reply was: "To see a friend."

"Oh," said Phillips. "You remind me of the Frenchman who received the same answer, and said, 'Take me along, I never saw one.'"

I often think a friend has to be brought up like a child, for this business of friend making is no small affair. Often it is well worth the thought and effort of a lifetime. As proof, ask the one who has come to the evening of life without one. At such a time, all the gathering of wealth or fame, or accumulation of this or that, cannot compensate for this one great loss of a friend.

Life presents many an experience of sorrow over the disappointment in friends. But there is joy in the persistent pursuit of a friend. The first step to gain a friend should be to believe in him, to recognize his failings — though they be as numberless as the sands of the sea, and to tie to his good traits though the former outnumber the latter, ten to one!

It was Stevenson who once wrote that "ten thousand bad traits cannot make a single good one any the <u>less</u> good."

To own a kindly smile, a cheerful outlook on life, an undying faith in the good intentions of others though ones own heart may be bathed in sorrow and cluttered with shattered dreams, is to present to the world an example of courage and character from which the chilled hands and heart of one hungering for a friend — lives may be warmed and spurred into happiness.

To gain a friend is to discover happiness — to keep a friend is be prepared for heaven.

Friendship #2 Writing

Friendship — was a darker passion than love. To be in love with a woman might buffet you with the power of something beyond control but it stretched you as no such rock as the imperious despotism of your feeling for a friend. That was a tyranny submerged and dark and contradictory, more unpredictable than angels or the weather, strange and uncharted, beyond logic, beyond guessing.

Friendship #3 Writing

A Friend's Greeting

I'd like to be the sort of friend that you have been to me;
I'd like to be the help that you've been always glad to be;
I'd like to mean as much to you each minute of the day
As you have meant, old friend of mine, to me along the way.

Friendship #4 Writing

I'd like to do the big things and the splendid things for you,
To brush the gray from out your skies, and leave them only blue.
I'd like to say the kindly things that I so oft have heard.
And feel that I could rouse your soul the way that mine you've stirred.

I'd like to give you back the joy that you have given me,
Yet that were wishing you a need I hope will never be;
I'd like to make you feel as rich as I who travel on
Undaunted in the darkest hours with you to lean upon.

I'm wishing at this Christmas time that I could but repay,
A portion of the gladness that you've strewn along my way.
And could I have one wish this year, this only would it be:
I'd like to be the sort of friend that you have been to me.

Quotes

"Bourgeois" is an epithet which the riffraff apply to what is respectable, and the aristocracy to what is decent."

"Economy is going without something you do want in case you should — some day — want something which you probably won't want."

"Marriages are made in heaven; I thought of waiting till I got there."

Names on the back of this sheet:

Mrs. A. Wintenfield

Radcliffe, Iowa

Mrs. Ben Word

Laredo, Mo

Tracked Events

1. Saw a Paramount-British movie with "Donnie" Hale, who appears with and is wedded to Jessie Mathews, the sensational British singer and dancing star.

2. Floyd T., the b. had evidently been there before, because when we had been seated, the orchestra played a medley of Southern tunes — Dixie, Swanee River, etc.

3. Joe E Brown — Fireman, Dave, my child met a friend of "Tommy's who lives in BG

4. Escudero, our favorite "garçon" the Ukraine had formerly lived and worked in Havana, and Tommy had known him there while spending his honeymoon in Cuba.

About Linda Flynn

Linda Flynn is a student of life. Life is the journey! She's interested in travel and understanding different cultures; people and relationships; natural beauty; creativity and how God works in these various aspects of existence. Writing presents opportunities to bring all these interests together.

Linda worked most of her career in technology, dreaming of the day when she'd find time to write something other than code, technical documents or business papers. Retired, she and her husband moved to the mountains of Colorado. There she's allowed her artistic side more freedom. She acknowledges the many and varied ways creativity is part of her life. She finds the muses of writing and the splendor of nature surrounding her as impetus for words that flow onto the page.

Stumbling upon these writings brings together many of the facets of Linda's lifestyle and interests. She found this work fascinating.

It has been an honor for her to give these writings new life.

You can check out what Linda's up to on her blog "JourneyToTheHeights.com," or find her other books on Amazon.com.

www.ingramcontent.com/pod-product-compliance
Lightning Source LLC
Chambersburg PA
CBHW041408010726
47507CB00001B/34

* 9 7 8 1 7 3 2 1 8 6 4 0 8 *